ABOUT THE *I*

CU00919354

When Geoffrey McSkim:
found an old motion-picture projector and a urn
containing a dusty film in his grandmother's attic.
He screened the film and was transfixed by
the flickering image of a man in a jaunty pith helmet,
baggy Sahara shorts and special desert sun-spectacles.
The man had an imposing macaw and a clever-looking
camel, and Geoffrey McSkimming was mesmerized
by their activities in black-and-white Egypt, Peru,
Greece, and other exotic locations.

Years later he discovered the identities of the trio,
and he has spent much of his time since then retracing
their footsteps, interviewing surviving members of the
Old Relics Society, and gradually reconstructing these
lost true tales which have become the enormously
successful Cairo Jim Chronicles.

Cairo Jim and the Alabastron of Forgotten Gods
was completed after Geoffrey McSkimming travelled
through Greece, piecing together what he considers
to be the most flabbergasting Cairo Jim tale yet!

For Belinda,
who felt the sleeting rains
and the snow-laced winds of
Samothraki upon her cheek and
who never once complained…

CAIRO JIM

AND THE ALABASTRON OF FORGOTTEN GODS

A Tale of Disposable Despicableness

GEOFFREY McSKIMMING

WALKER
BOOKS

First published in Great Britain 2006 by Walker Books Ltd
87 Vauxhall Walk, London SE11 5HJ

2 4 6 8 10 9 7 5 3 1

Text © 1996 Geoffrey McSkimming
Cover illustration © 2006 Martin Chatterton

This book has been typeset in Plantin

Printed in Great Britain by
Cox & Wyman Ltd, Reading, Berkshire

British Library Cataloguing in Publication Data:
a catalogue record for this book is available from the British Library.

ISBN-13: 978-1-4063-0022-2
ISBN-10: 1-4063-0022-5

www.walkerbooks.co.uk

▲▲▲▲▲ CONTENTS ▲▲▲▲▲

But in recent years, with nothing left worth seizing or destroying, there have been no more battles amid these wonderful ruins. Shattered, but serene, the temples calmly watch the centuries come and go. By day they smile at the tiny mortals, like ourselves, who crawl, awe-struck, over the mossy stones. And at night in the starlight these broken giants, very old, very lonely, and forgotten by the world, sleep and dream of their mighty past.

Richard Halliburton
Second Book of Marvels (1938)

TEMPERATURE'S RISING

"CONFOUND THESE Athenian summers!"

The very tall, very bulky, very sweaty woman put down her black Gladstone bag on the top step at the entrance to the Museum, and puffed out loudly. It was still only early in the day, but already the temperature had soared incredibly high, and the sunlight seemed to be dancing all about her in an excitable haze, quick-stepping here and cha-cha-ing there, to some silent rhythm of escalating hotness.

The woman took a deep breath and puffed out again, her large bosom heaving beneath her purple velvet frock. Above her left eyebrow – which looked like a muscly, dark caterpillar perched on her forehead – a plump bead of moisture appeared and began to trickle down, through the thick caterpillarian growth. The bead of moisture emerged from the underside of the hairy junglette, and trickled further, past the bulky woman's eye, onto her cheek, and still on, until it disappeared underneath her chartreuse-coloured yashmak – the heavy veil that covered the lower part of her face from under her nose to mid-way down her throat.

She reached into her pocket and withdrew a fine, yellow silk handkerchief, which she quickly used to dab at her chin underneath the veil. "I should've stayed put," she muttered. "If I'd've known it was going to be *this* hot, I'd never have ventured forth."

She wiped her forehead with the silk, and looked down her broad nose at her black bag. Then, for no apparent reason, she screwed up her nose and gave the bag a sharp kick with her heavy, though elegantly designed, boot.

The bag listed and fell onto its side with a dull *flump*ing sound.

The woman seemed to be calmed slightly by this action. She put the silk handkerchief back into her oven-like pocket and a small moan of pleasure came from behind the yashmak.

Lifting her eyes, she gazed out across the city of Athens, past the hotels and shops and speeding automobiles, and upwards to the great summit of the Acropolis. Even at this distance, the massive marble ruins of the Parthenon and the Temple of Athena Nike were gleaming in the sunlight, as white and brilliant as if they had been built only yesterday.

The woman gazed up at this, and a louder moan of pleasure, mixed with the urgency of her mission, escaped from under her veil.

"No, I *must* be here," she whispered to the faraway marble monuments, "I would still have come, even if the heat was such to melt the Arch of Hadrian. It is my *destiny*!"

A pattering of footsteps from behind halted her

whispers. She clenched her jaw and reined her desires and her secretive ambitions back in again, to a private place where they could not be heard.

"Doctor Hermione Dinkus, I presume?" came a voice.

The woman turned to face her greeter: a small man, pear-shaped in body – but not fat – with a head that seemed to be a tad oversized for his neck. On top of this head sat a little pile of lustrous black curls, which had been neatly combed and set into a tidy arrangement (as they had been day after day, year after year) with the help of some glossy hair lotion. The man wore a light blue suit and a dark blue necktie, and this combination of shades of the same colour set off his dark, twinkling eyes in an understated, simple, altogether modest way.

He lowered his head, a shy smile spreading across his lips. "Welcome to the National Archaeological Museum of Greece, Doctor Dinkus. As I said in my reply to your last letter, may I say what an honour – what a *thrill*, if you will pardon the expression – it is to have you visit us for your research."

"Thank you for fitting me in," said the woman, in a deep, formal tone. "I take it that you are—"

"Oh! Forgive me! I am a little ... how do I put it ... fluttered."

Doctor Hermione Dinkus raised her caterpillarian growths at him quizzically.

"No, I am sorry, I mean *flustered*." The man put his hand to his mouth and quietly cleared his throat.

"Allow me to introduce myself formally: I am the Keeper of the Museum's Gallery of Forgotten Gods. Euripides Doodah."

"Euripides Doodah? Euripides, eh? My, oh my, what a wonderful day," said Hermione Dinkus dryly.

Euripides Doodah rolled his eyes; he had heard *that* jest many times during his life. He gave his usual courteous chuckle, though, the one he usually gave whenever someone made the jest, as if this was the first time that anybody had ever said it to him. "Ah, that is very witty, Doctor Dinkus. Yes, it *is* a wonderful day, despite this incredible heat."

"I feel like I am melting on the spot," Hermione Dinkus gasped, as another fat droplet of perspiration began its cross-country expedition down the territory of her face.

"Let us enter the Museum," said Euripides Doodah. "You will find the temperature much lower inside. All of our beautiful white marble statues give off such an aura of coolness; they act as natural air-conditioners. They keep the place almost nippy, in fact."

"I'm certainly pleased to hear *that*."

She stooped to pick up her Gladstone, but before her thick fingers had made contact with the handle, the bag was whisked away by Euripides Doodah. "Please, Doctor Dinkus, allow me."

"No, thank you, Mr Doodah, *I* will take my bag."

"I will not hear of it," Euripides Doodah smiled. "In my country, the gentleman always—"

"*I will take my bag!*" whispered Hermione Dinkus, in such a burst of hushed threateningness that the pile of curls on Euripides Doodah's head quivered.

He handed the Gladstone back to her promptly. "Of course, Doctor Dinkus. Forgive me, please."

Hermione Dinkus clutched the black bag close to her bosom. "Now let us enter your great Museum," she suggested. "There is *much* I have to do."

Euripides Doodah, the Keeper of the Gallery of Forgotten Gods, had been right: it was vastly cooler – almost nippy, in fact – inside the massive walls of the Archaeological Museum.

He and Hermione Dinkus, Doctor of Archaeological Studies and fully-fledged Member of the Old Relics Society in Cairo, Egypt, walked briskly along the shiny marble floors. Their footsteps – his light and eager, hers heavy and purposeful – echoed loudly as they made their way through the interior of the magnificent building.

"Exactly how far is it to the Gallery of Forgotten Gods?" she asked after a few clip-clopping minutes.

"A little way more," he answered in a sad voice.

"It's certainly a long way from the entrance," she grumbled. "I don't imagine that many visitors would feel like making the trek all the way down *here*."

"No, Doctor Dinkus, you are right on that score. We don't get many visitors to the Gallery of Forgotten Gods. Not any more. We *used* to, quite a few years ago now, when the Forgotten Gods collection of antiquities was located closer to the Museum's entrance, but ever since it was moved back here ... well..." he gave a loud sigh, "I suppose people will only walk *so* far to seek out the past."

"They relocated the Gallery?"

"Yes, about eight or nine years ago." He gave a wistful smile, but his eyes told a different story. "It is peculiar, is it not, how in only eight or nine years such forgetfulness can set in? We need replenishment of people's memories, Doctor Dinkus. Nowadays *nobody* seems to remember this part of our history..."

"Nobody but us, Mr Doodah. Nobody but us."

"Exactly. Another score upon which you are correct. It is *so* exciting that you are going to include a whole chapter on the old gods in your new book ... what is it entitled again?"

"*Dust Never Sleeps*", replied Hermione Dinkus proudly.

"That's right, I remember now. You wrote it in your third letter to me. Forgive my memory, I am a bit ... how do you say it? Scanty sometimes."

She looked at him quizzically.

"No, I mean, *scatty*."

"That's all right, soon the title will be on everybody's lips. You mark my words, Mr Doodah, the book will be a volume of immense archaeological significance."

"There is no doubt in my head of *that*."

On they walked, echoingly and urgently, past galleries and rooms filled with countless white marble statues staring unblinkingly at the noisy hordes of tourists, students and other sundry visitors who were gradually filling the place.

(Not all of the statues were able to stare out at their visitors, as a good number had lost their heads – and other assorted limbs and appendages – at various stages throughout their histories.)

With every gallery that Hermione Dinkus and Euripides Doodah passed, however, the boisterous crowds seemed to decrease; the number of statues did not. Nor did the beautiful ancient vases, formed in many different and once practical shapes – jars for mixing liquids (known as kraters), water jugs (hydrias), drinking cups (rhytons), oil and perfume flasks (alabastra and lekythoi) – many of them painted intricately with bold black-and-orange or white-and-black designs and scenes from ancient legends.

Equally as plentiful were the finely turned small pots; the handsome ancient theatre masks, grimacing tragically or laughing wildly; the splendid, tiled mosaics and wall paintings that had once lain and hung resplendent on the floors and walls of long-gone temples and the homes of the wealthy; the thousands of tiny yet perfectly sculpted bronze statuettes of gods, humans, animals and monsters; the golden death masks and burial jewellery found at Mycenae. There were enough pieces of antiquity in this establishment to make a visitor dizzy.

Presently the Doctor and the Keeper had walked such a distance that they encountered no other people at all – only the white, silent, shining statues of men and women, gods and goddesses, horses and centaurs, children, senators and citizens, sirens and sphinxes, some of them limbless and all of them loitering as they kept solitary vigil over everything around them.

Euripides Doodah felt a great inner tingle spreading slowly down his spine, a tingle full of calm and peacefulness. This lonely section of the Museum always made him feel at rest, despite (or was it because of?) the fact that it was largely ignored by the intruding sightseers.

"Surely we are almost there?" Hermione Dinkus questioned, her large fingers clutching her Gladstone tightly to her bust.

"Surely we are, Doctor Dinkus. This way, if you please." He turned the very next corner, and she followed with clumping footsteps.

"On behalf of the Archaeological Museum of Greece, I welcome you to the Gallery of Forgotten Gods. The gods who came, who ruled the earth and the seas and the skies, before the Olympians!"

Doctor Hermione Dinkus looked from the twinkling eyes of Euripides Doodah to the small, high-ceilinged room which they had entered. She scanned the single, tall display case made of glass and mahogany wood that was fixed to the wall furthest from her. Upon the shelves within, protected by the heavy glass barrier of the display case's door, was a neatly arranged collection of small vases, pieces of statuary, pottery shards and several miniature, replicated models of temples and shrines, the real versions of which had once, long ago, been important in the worship of the old gods, but had long since crumbled to nothing.

At both sides of this display case, two imposing columns had been positioned, having been removed from a timeworn Thracian site on an island in the north of Greece.

Hermione Dinkus loosened her grasp on the handles of her bag and slowly stooped to lower it to the floor, turning her broad back to Euripides Doodah as she did so. She set the bag firmly on the cool white marble – he thought he heard her give a small *squawk*, which he thought was an odd sound for such an esteemed woman to make – and she straightened again. Then she turned to face him once more, standing in front of the bag.

"There is one particular object," she said, in a voice full of desire and intensity, "that I wish above all others to behold. I will make a feature of it in my chapter on the Forgotten Gods in *Dust Never Sleeps*." Her chartreuse yashmak quivered expectantly.

"I think I know what that object might be," Euripides Doodah whispered loudly. "Would it by any chance be … the Sacred Alabastron of Cronus?"

"Bingo, boyo!" exclaimed the woman gravely.

Euripides Doodah took a step forwards, but then quickly stepped backwards again; his first instinct – to give the Doctor a huge hug – was, perhaps, not the best instinct, in view of her powerful size and her displayed abrupt manner. So instead he whispered again, with great and respectful excitement, "Oh, Doctor Dinkus! You are going to feature one of our most important, one of our most neglected, one of our most *legendary* objects. One that so many generations of scholars and historians have forgotten about, one that was believed to be" – and here he winked theatrically at her – "singularly responsible for setting in motion the fates that paved the way for the Olympian Gods, who in their exalted heyday—"

He stopped suddenly, his last word hanging in the echoing air as he looked sharply around. "*What was that sound, Doctor Dinkus?*"

Hermione Dinkus's heavy eyebrows scuttled down towards her eyes. "What sound?" she hissed. "I heard nothing, Mr Doodah."

"A *clicking* sound, short but loud. Like something being opened."

"I heard no click, sir."

"I definitely did. It pierced my concentration. Let me look around—"

He went to approach the display case behind her, but Hermione Dinkus opened her arms, her purple velvet frock spreading as wide as a pair of theatre curtains on an enormous stage. "I think you are hearing imaginary things, Mr Doodah. I heard nothing, nothing at all. And I have perfect hearing, I have only recently had my ears seen to. Maybe it is the heat getting to you. Maybe you had a *fata morgana*★ of the earholes."

★ Mirage

"No, no, the heat is not affecting me, I am accustomed to days such as—"

"The heat has certainly got to *me*," the large woman interrupted. "Oh, Heavens to the Goddess Betsy, yes. In fact, I have come over colossally faint all of a sudden. I wonder if you would be so kind as to procure me a glass of water?" A plump bead of perspiration plopped down onto her yashmak.

"Water?" said Euripides Doodah, still listening for a return of the mysterious clicking sound.

Her yashmak blew out as she exhaled sharply. "Oh, I think I am struggling for breath… Please, Mr Doodah, I would throw away my professional reputation for a single glass of water!"

"Yes, yes," panicked the worried gentleman, "of course you shall have your water. But that sound I heard—"

"Have no fear, sir, while you are fetching me my liquid salvation, I will stand guard over this Gallery. Nothing shall intrude without my knowing!"

"Thank you, Doctor—"

"Please, *water*!"

"At once, at once!" He turned and sped off around the corner.

The only good thing that had come from the Gallery of Forgotten Gods being moved to the back extremities of the Museum was that it was now a much shorter walk for Euripides Doodah whenever he needed to use the Kitchen of the Keepers. This greatly suited him, as one of his chief pleasures in life – apart from his beloved

Gallery of antiquities – was drinking cups of strong black coffee with marshmallows melted in them. Sometimes in the old days, especially in the mornings, his need for a cup of coffee with melted marshmallows in it had been so strong that he had almost had to run whenever he wanted to make it; the Kitchen had been so far away, and every moment without coffee with marshmallows in it was nearly unbearable. But being a gentleman, Euripides Doodah never, ever, ran inside the Museum, and so the journey to the Kitchen had always been a trek of gruelling endurance. Now that the distance between Kitchen and Gallery was much less torturous, he was able to walk it with calmness and certainty, no matter how parched his throat, no matter how great his craving.

It was along this route that he now strode rapidly, down the long, statue-lined corridor, through the door bearing the sign NO ADMITTANCE – MUSEUM STAFF ONLY, turning left and into the Staff Tea Room, before arriving at the Kitchen of the Keepers.

He went briskly to the sink, selected a drinking glass from the shelf above and turned on the tap. The water sloshed fiercely and filled the glass to overflowing. He drained off some of the water, then wiped the bottom of the glass with a Museum Teatowel.

Back he strode, out of the Staff Tea Room, out through the door bearing the sign, NO ADMITTANCE – MUSEUM STAFF ONLY, along the statue-lined corridor, on and on, his footsteps slapping loudly against the silence of all the ancient artistry around him. He was careful to spill as little of the water as possible.

At last he came to the part of the corridor that contained the entrance to the Gallery of Forgotten Gods. He gripped the drinking glass tightly in his sweating fingers – why they were sweaty, he knew not – and ventured into his most favourite place in the modern world.

What Euripides Doodah saw upon entering the silent, tranquil Gallery made the pile of curls on the top of his head quiver with a dread that his follicles had never before known.

He dropped what he was carrying.

It hurtled onto the marble floor in a cannon-blast explosion of glass and water that was surely, definitely, *horrifyingly* shocking enough to wake the dead of many centuries past.

2

A CALL TO CAIRO JIM

"BRIIIING, BRIIIING! Akka-akka-akka. Briiiing, briiiing!"

The small field telephone rang with an impertinence that was completely out of place in the otherwise calm and sedate Valley of the Kings in Upper Egypt.

Inside his modest and much-patched tent, Cairo Jim – that well-known archaeologist and little-known poet – jumped in alarm. A dollop of shaving-lather fell from his chin and spattered onto his left Sahara boot.

"RAAAARK! RERRAAAARK!" came another burst of noise from outside, even louder than that of the field telephone. Jim jumped again, another dollop of lather flying off the tip of his nose and hitting his circular shaving-mirror. He quickly wiped his face with his shaving-towel and, pausing only to put on his special desert sun-spectacles and pith helmet, hurried out through the partly-opened flap of the tent.

"Raaaark!" screeched Doris, the learned and brave macaw who was Cairo Jim's indispensable companion. She was hopping up and down on the end of her perch-stand, frantically opening and closing her huge, yellow-and-blue wings, as she glared balefully at the telephone.

|᠁| 20 |᠁|

"*Briiiing, briiiing! Akka-akka-akka. Briiiing, briiiing!*"

"*Raaaaaaaaark!*"

"There, there, Doris, my dear," soothed Jim. "It's probably only Gerald Perry Esquire calling from the Old Relics Society. It's usually only ever him."

"Infernal machine," spluttered the macaw. "I don't know how he ever persuaded you to get it ensconced down here."

"It's so he can get in touch with me quickly, in case anything perplexing crops up."

"*Briiiing, briiiing!*"

"It's an intrusion, that's what it is," Doris squawked, a scowl curling around the edges of her beak. "Let's drop it in a bucket of water and be done with it. 'Insolent noise-maker, we are less afraid to be drowned than thou art.'"

Jim gave her a strange look.

"*The Tempest*, by Mr Shakespeare," blinked the bird. "Act One, Scene One, spoken by Antonio, if you want to be precise."

"Very good, Doris."

Sitting over by the tent, Brenda the Wonder Camel (Cairo Jim's other indispensable companion) lifted her long-lashed eyes from her new Western adventure novel – *Melodious Tex and the Clue of the Crying Cactus* – and regarded her two friends and the intrusive field telephone with an air of bemusement that was common to camels from the Wonder Herd of Thebes. She gave a quiet snort – "Quaaooo" – and returned to her book,

keeping one ear open just in case the telephone call would prove to be interesting.

"*Briiiing, briiiing!*"

"Reraark! Answer it, please, Jim, before I go off the twig." Doris blinked her small dark eyes again. "I mean, the perch."

"Yes, I suppose I'd better."

He took a deep breath and had a small shudder (he had found that in the short time in which they had shared their campsite with the field telephone, he didn't actually enjoy talking on it very much at all). Then, with an admirable sense of duty, he picked up the heavy brown receiver and put it gently to his ear.

"Hello?" he said loudly, in his clear "telephone" voice. "This is Jim speaking."

"Who is it?" screeched Doris, flapping her wings and lifting slightly off the perch.

Jim cupped his hand over the mouthpiece. "It's Perry, just as we'd thought. Don't worry, my dear, he probably only wants to talk to me about the poem I sent him for the Society's June newsletter. You remember, the one entitled 'Desert Inkling, Stars A-Tinkling'."

Doris remembered it only too well: she rolled her eyes and wrinkled the edges around her beak.

The archaeologist-poet spoke into the receiver again. "Hello, Perry, so what did you think of the poetry? Did you like the line about the sands of the desert being like a mildly relentless, never-ending realm of sandpaper? I know I was especially pleased with—"

"Jim!" Gerald Perry Esquire's voice burst down the line like a crackling gunshot. "I'm not telephoning about the poem."

"Oh." Cairo Jim did his best not to sound disappointed.

"No, it's something far worse than that. *Much* more dire. Something of the darkest consequence for the world of antiquities has taken place!"

Jim pushed the brim of his pith helmet further up his forehead. "Go on, Perry, I'm listening."

Doris, seeing the lines of concentration emerging above Jim's special desert sun-spectacles, quietened down and gazed at him intently. Brenda, sensing that something was askew in the world of human beings, gently closed her book with her snout and remained at the ready.

"It's a theft, Jim," crackled Perry. "From the Archaeological Museum in Athens. They fear it could be the theft of the millennia!"

A line of heavy beads of perspiration broke out on the top of Jim's upper lip and stayed there, motionless, as if it too wanted to hear more. "What was taken?" he asked.

"An alabastron," Perry answered, his voice thick with static and solemnity.

"An alabastron? Is that all? Why, Perry, there are tons of them in Greece, and all around the world for that matter. How can a single alabastron—?"

"What's an alabastron?" squawked Doris impatiently.

"A small, narrow-necked vase without handles, often

used in ancient Greece as a perfume container," thought Brenda, who had retained a vast knowledge of factual information ever since she had accidentally eaten twenty-seven volumes of the *Encyclopaedia Britannica* when she had been an inquisitive calf.

Her thought travelled across the hot desert air that lay between her and Jim. He put his hand over the mouthpiece and spoke to Doris. "It's a small, narrow-necked vase without handles, often used in ancient Greece as a perfume container."

"Raark," said Doris. "I live and learn."

"I'm sorry, Perry, yes, I'm still here. I was saying, I don't see how the theft of a single alabastron can be so very catastrophic. For the love of Zeus, there are thousands—"

"That's what I thought, too, at first," interrupted Perry. "Just another ancient vase. But there's more to it than that, Jim. Much more. Apparently the Governors of the Museum in Athens know a few things about this particular alabastron that we don't. They've gone into a frightful tizz over its disappearance. They've asked whether you and Doris and Brenda might be able to give them a hand, wing and hoof to get to the bottom of the whole nefarious incident."

"We certainly will," Jim answered without hesitation. When it came to the plunder of antiquities, wild donkeys couldn't keep him from trying to right the wrong.

"Good on you, Jim. We at the Old Relics Society knew we could depend on you. Now don't worry about a thing – I'll make sure you've got enough Greek drachmas to keep all of you going while you're away, and you can put any big expenses down to me here at the Society."

"Thank you, Perry, as usual you're a champion."

"Yes," crackled Perry, who knew that facts like that should be stated once in a while. "Now, listen, I'm sending one of those new-fangled helicopter thingummies down to collect you and Doris and Brenda – she might have to breathe in a little, Jim, it's a good thing she's double-jointed – and whisk you straight up to Athens."

"A helicopter?"

"Mmm, been using one to advertise m' newest take-away pigeon deal for m' restaurants. Great gimmick, y'know. We've got this banner that trails from the back of the thing, 'Perry's Prized Pigeon Portions – Perfect, Prompt, Pleasurable Plus Plump' it reads, it's a longish banner, and I fly around with the pilot of the helicopter thingummy and a big bag full of cooked pigeon between m' legs. Then when we're over a public place where there are lots of people doing nothing of great consequence, I open the door and toss the cuisine up into the blades of the 'copter. They slice it into convenient bite-sized pieces that shower down onto the people doing nothing of great consequence below. Instant diced delicacies!"

Jim's stomach felt strangely turbulent for some reason.

"Anyway, the helicopter should arrive at your camp in about half an hour. You'll find everything you'll need from me, on the back seat. Now, off you go and pack – there isn't much time, you know."

"Yes, er, I—"

"All the biggest success to you, Jim. And to Doris and Brenda. Remember, the archaeological world is counting on you. Not to mention the modern world, these things are often intertwined, aren't they? Must dash, it's the Society's Biannual Yodelling Championships starting up tonight – I've got to go and see Ladislav Inglis and get fitted for lederhosen and a little green hat with a feather in. I think I'll get *embroidered* braces on the lederhosen this time. The judges like those best, and they flatter my legs. The braces, not the judges. Cheerio!"

The line went dead, and Jim replaced the receiver, hoping as he did so that he'd have as much energy when he was an old man as Gerald Perry Esquire did.

"What's up, then?" Doris questioned, her crest feathers arching forward.

"Well, gang, it looks like we're off to Greece."

"Quaaaoo!" Brenda fluttered her eyelashes expectantly.

"Reraark," squawked Doris, hopping up and down on her perch. "Off to the cradle of civilisation, are we?"

"You bet your barbules," said Jim.

"Because of this vase thing?"

"It's an alabastron, Doris. Come on." He held out his

arm, and the beautiful bird fluttered up and off her perch and came to land gracefully next to Jim's Cutterscrog Old Timers Archaeological Timepiece on his wrist. "And I'll tell you all about it while we're packing. Brenda, my lovely, could you check out the travelling condition of your double-seated saddle while we're getting our things together? We might need the extra room, you never know."

"Quaaooo," snorted the Wonder Camel, rolling her huge head in a circular motion.

Jim smiled, and he and Doris disappeared into the tent.

Brenda swished her tail and rose on her spindly but strong legs. In her typical, always silent, mostly calm way, she lumbered to where, behind the tent, her double-seated saddle lay in the shadowy sand. She nudged it with her snout, turned it over and began checking that all of the straps were securely attached, and that the ornate macramé covering was still in good enough condition for another expedition.

After a few minutes of inspectful prodding she lifted her head and cocked it in the direction of a far-off, as yet *unfelt* breeze, as she listened to the distant whirring sound – still hundreds of miles away – that was to very soon scatter the sands wildly around her and Doris and Jim.

🔲🔲🔲🔲🔲 3 🔲🔲🔲🔲🔲

TO THE CRADLE...

THE SANDS WERE SCATTERED by a million bursts of wind; the flying contraption arrived, heralded by its own blare; moving quickly, Jim, Doris and Brenda raced, crouching and hovering low, to the rear compartment. The helicopter blades continued to rotate slowly and lurchingly.

Jim yanked open the door and, holding down his pith helmet with his other hand, he hurled his bulging knapsack and tightly wrapped black umbrella inside. Then he and Doris squeezed Brenda onto the back seat and pressed her saddle and themselves in after her.

The archaeologist-poet slammed the door shut and gave the thumbs-up signal. From the front of the helicopter, the pilot returned the signal and the blades above them began to speed up. As they did so, the noise swelled, rising over the passengers like a bursting wave – *terka-terka-terka-terka* – and the vehicle started to shake.

"Jim!" Doris scrambled to the back of Jim's seat, to a position comfortably close to his pith helmet and neck. "Is it safe?"

He reached back and tousled her crest reassuringly. "Have no fear, my dear. We'll be fine."

"It's only that *I* don't vibrate like this when *I* fly."

"Quaaoo!" Brenda, scrunched hard against the far door (it *was* a good thing she was double-jointed), seemed to share Doris's uncertainty. She squirmed her humps nervously.

"There, there, my lovely," Jim said to her, "we'll all settle down once we're airborne."

"I hope so," squawked Doris.

Then, in little more than a breath of a second, they all soared forward, encased within their metal surroundings, and up, up and up, and now the sands were no longer anywhere near them. The shaking continued, but gradually became less unsettling. Soon their campsite – Jim's tent, Doris's perch, Brenda's "special" patch of sand, all of their wooden crates and barrels full of provisions and distractions and diversions – was nothing but a dot, shrinking and hazing before their eyes, until it became a mere speck that merged into the endless orange desert below.

Jim looked away from his now invisible home, and sighed. The pores of skin at the back of his neck tingled, zinging to life the way they always did whenever the promise of a looming challenge and a new archaeological undertaking came his way. He began to smile, but all at once the smile became a grimace, as something quite unwelcome made itself known to his nether portions.

"Ooh, what a pain in the…" He wriggled and lifted the eastern side of his posterior from the leather seat. Reaching down, he withdrew the object that had caused his bottom to react in a mixture of pain and intrigue: a medium-sized, slightly scuffed, brass-buckled leather satchel, which bore the faded gold initials "G.P. Esq."

"Rark! What's inside?" inquired Doris.

"You can open it if you want to."

Doris hopped down onto the satchel and smugly began to undo the buckles with her beak (she always liked it when Jim let her do the unveilings). When she had accomplished this, she hopped back to her spot near his shoulder and looked down.

Brenda twisted her neck so that she, too, could glimpse the contents.

Cairo Jim reached into the satchel and took out a loose bundle of documents. There was a large, folded map of the entire country of Greece, including all of the islands; an envelope containing enough Greek drachmas to last them for several weeks; a photograph of a blonde-haired, heavily eyelashed nightclub entertainer named Fifi Glusac who was flashing an unnatural number of teeth in her mouth and an unequally unnatural number of sequins on her frock (Jim had no idea why *this* was in the satchel, and Gerald Perry Esquire would wonder for a long time where it had got to); the latest newsletter of the Old Relics Society; and a very good bit of string. Jim did not need any explanation for the latter's inclusion, as there had long been a maxim in the Society that "you never know when you'll need a good bit of string".

There was also a single sheet of neatly folded papyrus,

on which Gerald Perry's spidery handwriting informed them that firstly and most importantly they should contact Euripides Doodah, the Keeper of the Gallery of Forgotten Gods at the Archaeological Museum in Athens.

The archaeologist-poet placed all the bits and pieces into a neat pile and slid them back into the satchel. "It appears that Perry's looking after us in his usual style," he smiled at his friends.

"Reerraarrk!" screeched Doris.

"Quaaooo!" snorted Brenda.

For the next half hour or so they all flew in their own silence, as the noise made it hard to hold a decent sort of conversation in this aircraft. Each of them became full of their own thoughts and ponderings...

While being very eager to reach Athens, the closer Jim got, the more annoyed he became – annoyed that yet another piece of the world's antiquity had been stolen. He stared out through his desert sun-spectacles into the breadth of sky outside, and imagined just what he'd do if – *when* – he got his hands on whoever was irresponsibly responsible...

Doris was absorbed in her thoughts about Greece. She didn't know a great deal about this country to which she had not yet paid a visit, only things that she had read from those plays by Mr William Shakespeare that were set there. She recalled their titles as she blinked in the bright sunlight: *A Midsummer Night's Dream*, bits of *Troilus and Cressida*, *Timon of Athens*, bits of *Pericles, Prince of Tyre*, *The Two Noble Kinsmen*. Would the Greece of today be the same as when Mr Shakespeare had written about it? She prowked quietly to herself as she dwelled on this...

Brenda was concentrating on trying not to let her humps tingle, as that was something she enjoyed almost as much as grains of sand flying up her nostrils if she hadn't closed them off in time. She sat, like a humped squeeze-box, and – to distract her thoughts from her humps – contemplated the inner workings of escalators, those mechanical marvels invented to convey human beings with a minimum of fuss and effort.

Eventually Doris got bored with thinking about the Grecian plays of Shakespeare. She hopped across the back of the seat and settled herself near Brenda's snout.

"How about the *game* again?" she asked close to Brenda's ear, so that only Brenda, and not Jim, could hear her.

Brenda, with reluctance bristling through her mane, squinted at Doris.

"Come on, Bren, we haven't played it for days. He hasn't cottoned on to it yet."

The Wonder Camel looked out of the corner of her eye at Jim, then at Doris's pleading featherbrows, then back at Jim again. "Quaaaoo!" she agreed. It *was* fun, this game that Doris had invented, and it *would* help pass the time.

"Rark, you fun-filled Beast of Wonder! I'll go first." She hopped down and across to Jim's knee, which protruded from his baggy Sahara shorts.

He looked down and smiled. "Hello, there."

"Rerk," she answered, rolling her wings at the shoulders in a gesture of friendship which she saved exclusively for Cairo Jim. Before he was able to look away from her, she opened her beak wide, as wide as it would go without it thwanging up and into her face.

Then she snapped it swiftly shut.

Jim blinked heavily.

Doris's eyes crinkled at the edges.

After a few moments, Jim looked across to Brenda.

As soon as she saw his gaze fixed on her, she, too, opened her jaws wide. She let them hang open for four seconds or so, after which they sprang shut again.

The archaeologist-poet blinked once more. He stretched his back against the leather of the seat behind him.

Doris hopped up so that she was between Jim and Brenda. This time when he looked at the macaw (and there wasn't any way he *couldn't* have looked at her in that position, for she was very close indeed), she opened her mandibles so wide that he could almost see all the way down her throat.

Until, of course, she snapped them shut again.

Jim pulled off his sun-spectacles and gently rubbed his left eye with the back of his hand.

When he stopped this, Brenda caught his attention. She separated her jaws one more time into a gaping trough of tongue and camel teeth and Bactrian tonsils. But only for a carefully measured amount of time, whereupon she clamped them shut again.

 33

Doris watched Jim carefully.

So did Brenda.

Terka-terka-terka-terka went the helicopter's blades.

Jim took a deep breath and started to turn away from them to face the window, when Doris (not to be outdone) gave an urgent screech.

Jim looked at her immediately.

With indulgent measure, she raised her beak and opened it, until it could very well have been a huge chasm opening up to swallow the heavens surrounding them. Then – SNAP! – her beak shut.

And now, the moment Doris and Brenda had been waiting for: Cairo Jim opened his own mouth and took a long, much-needed, undeniably contagious, *yawn*.

Doris shot around the cabin, like a feathered balloon that might have just had its air let out suddenly. "Raaark! Reerraarrk!" She fluttered close to Brenda's ear. "There, you see? I won again!"

"Well swoggle me politely with a pillow," muttered Jim. "I feel so tired. How strange."

The Wonder Camel gave a small snort and smiled. She was glad that her plumed pal was able to find so much amusement at twenty thousand feet in the air.

On they flew, along the course of the river Nile and its lush green delta, over wadis and oases, further northward until below them appeared the mighty Sphinx and the magnificent pyramids of the Giza Plateau.

The sprawling city of Cairo was underneath them for

the briefest of minutes, then there was coastline and then, water. Water and water and water.

Presently they saw islands of interesting shape and colouring. Some of them were ringed by darkly sanded coastlines, and had high, craggy craters of ancient volcanoes at their centres.

Very soon the helicopter was approaching Athens. As the noisy blades spun above his head, Cairo Jim's poetry cells seemed to spin as well. The rhythm of the blades seeped into him, *terka-terka-terka-terka*, and a verse came swiftly to his mind:

> Accurséd be the plunder
> that plagues our ancient lands!
> A thousand peals of thunder
> should fall on these brigands
> who swipe archaic beauty
> and smuggle it abroad,
> then sell their precious looty
> for despicable reward!

He knew that "beauty" and "looty" were not the best bits of rhyme he had ever come up with but, at this moment, that didn't matter – there were far graver rhythms out in the world to worry about.

4

MUSEUM OF CALAMITY

THE HELICOPTER LANDED rapidly at a small helicopter pad on the outskirts of Athens. In an urgent muddle – and being extremely careful not to get Brenda's humps wedged in the narrow doorway – the trio disembarked, pulling Jim's satchel, umbrella and knapsack, as well as Brenda's saddle, out after them.

The pilot gave them a shadowy wave and, at the flick of a switch, the 'copter's blades gathered speed. The colossal noise rose again, and the aircraft lifted sharply into the sky.

Brenda bent her head low as the mechanical marvel disappeared. Doris, perched on the Wonder Camel's nether hump, kept her eye on the diminishing craft. "Commotional contraption," she squawked, her beak creased around the edges. "The day I get into another one of *those* is the day I get my feathers permed and start calling myself a poodle! Raark!"

Cairo Jim, who had been squatting by his knapsack, stood and held out his compass. He flipped open the protective lid and studied the dial. "Right, gang, the Museum should be due north-east. Let's get galloping."

"Quaaooo," snorted Brenda. She gripped one of the leather straps of her saddle and lifted it to Jim. "We have

 36

an alabastron to pursue," she thought in her telepathic way.

Jim took the saddle from her and, throwing it onto her humps, started to fasten the buckles and strappings around her. "We have an alabastron to pursue," he said worriedly.

"Funny," said Doris. "I was just about to squawk those very words myself."

Brenda galloped skilfully through the streets of Athens, dodging the automobiles and the many small, motorized bicycles that swerved in and out around each other like swarms of noisy, demented bees. The crowded heat, rising off the tarred roadways in shimmering vapours, soon made Jim's shirt stick wetly to his chest and back.

Even Doris, perched for dear life on Brenda's fore hump just in front of Jim's stomach, quickly had her feathers drenched as though someone had poured a bucket of water over her.

After nearly half an hour, Jim turned Brenda into Patission Street. She slowed her pace as she took the corner, then increased it again, and two minutes later Jim steered her off the street and into the front grounds of the National Archaeological Museum.

"Whoa, my lovely," he cried, bringing her to a stop in front of the marble steps.

"Rark." Doris shook out the feathers of her wings and blinked the dust from her eyes. "Good ride, Brenda."

The Wonder Camel fluttered her eyelashes in an it's-all-part-of-the-service sort of way, but her mane bristled with the pleasure of being appreciated.

Jim dismounted, and Doris fluttered across to land on his shoulder. The three of them looked up at the gigantic neo-classical building, with its columned portico and its four huge golden statues standing majestically on the roof.

"My friends," said Jim quietly, his spine tingling with the special kind of thrilling anticipation it always tingled with whenever he was about to enter another of the world's great keeping-places of treasure from ancient times, "this is one of the most exhilarating places we could ever hope to visit. You'll long remember what you will behold inside here. To think that some ... *felon* has dared to infiltrate these walls and—"

"Jim, look!" Doris fluttered by his ear, pointing with her right wing.

"By Rameses," muttered Jim, observing the small, agitated figure at the top of the stairs. Back and forth this figure strode, faster and faster, like someone in a film where the speed has been set way too high. "I've never seen a man pacing so quickly in all my days."

"He'll wear out the marble at the rate he's going," said the macaw.

"It's a wonder we can't see smoke coming from under his shoes," thought Brenda with a flick of her tail.

All at once the figure stopped and looked down at them. Its hands were flung momentarily into the air above the small, compact pile of curls on the top of its head, and Jim, Doris and Brenda heard a tiny sound coming from its throat – a sound of anxious pleasure, it seemed.

Then the figure came hurtling down the steps, arms outstretched, and grabbed the right hand of Jim and shook it earnestly.

"I *know* you are Jim of Cairo," blurted Euripides Doodah. "I recognize you from your photograph in the pages of the Old Relics Society newsletter. And I am *so* glad you have come. Your friend from the Society, Gerald Perry Esquire, advised me of your arrayal."

Jim, Doris and Brenda looked at him quizzically.

"Er, I mean, *arrival*." He paused and frowned. "Oh, please forgive me, forgive my confusion with these words. I am quite inside myself." Another pause, and this time a frown that almost turned his face upside-down. "I mean, *beside* myself."

"Certainly," said Jim, trying to extricate his hand from the vigorous, pumping grip of Euripides Doodah. "I quite understand, Mr— ?"

"Oh, pardon me. I am always forgetting introductionary courtesies. Doodah. Euripides Doodah."

Cairo Jim freed his hand from the nervous man's grasp and looked into his distressed, dark eyes. "Pleased to make your acquaintance. Perry told us to find you. It is, Mr Doodah, anything *but* a wonderful day."

Euripides lifted an anxiety-ridden eyebrow, then lowered it quickly. From Jim's response, Doodah realized that Cairo Jim had two very important things in his favour: an ear for words and a real passion for the plight that lay before them. In that one comment, Jim had revealed himself as a man to be trusted.

"You are absolutely correct, Cairo Jim," said the Keeper of the Gallery of Forgotten Gods. "It is a day to be dealt with, and I surely hope that Fate will deal us a hand of Victory!"

"I'd like you to meet my colleagues: Doris, who has a vast knowledge of the works of William Shakespeare and a great talent for deciphering ancient languages—"

"Epigraphy's my speciality," cooed Doris, extending her wing for Doodah to shake.

"—and Brenda," continued Jim, "who is from the Wonder Herd of Thebes, and who is spectacularly gifted in all manner of ways."

"Quaaooo," snorted the Wonder Camel, fluttering her eyelashes and lifting her front left hoof.

Euripides bowed his head and gave the hoof a courteous tug. "I am delightful. Now, let us enter the Museum and go to the Gallery. Time, I fear, could be plotting against us, and it is nearly half an hour since I last had a cup of coffee with marshmallows in it." He took from his pocket a large silver key – so large that he almost needed both hands to hold it. Then, followed by Jim, Doris and Brenda, he climbed the stairs to the massive iron doors, where he carefully inserted the key in the lock.

"Strange," Jim remarked as Euripides jiggled the key.

"There's nobody around but us. I thought the place would be bustling."

"Normally it is," Euripides informed him. "But since this heinous theft, the Museum Governors have decided to close the Museum until the alabastron is found again."

This struck Jim as a sad thing to do, but he remained silent. He removed his pith helmet and special desert sun-spectacles and stood, waiting.

Doodah turned the key. There was a loud unlocking sound, and he pushed one of the doors open. "Please, follow me," he said, and disappeared inside.

Jim, with Doris perched on his shoulder and Brenda following closely, did as instructed, and the door was closed behind them all.

Mr Doodah led the way, striding off in his brisk yet gentlemanly gait, and the others trailed after him, trying to keep up but also trying hard to resist the temptation of slowing down – and even stopping – to look at the beautiful marble and bronze statues. Gallery after Gallery was filled with them – statues of priests and priestesses, draped in multi-folded marble cloths; figures of goddesses; enormous monuments of muscled warriors (called kouroi) as tall as houses; heads of philosophers and wrestlers; busts of youths and old men; sirens; boys on porpoises; gigantic winged representations of Nike, the Goddess of Victory; countless gravestones, all of them beautifully carved with the images of the dead people they protected.

The marble statuary ranged in colour from clean

white to creamy mottledness to a dingy, greyish pallor, depending on the condition of the marble and how it had aged through the centuries.

"This ancient world, frozen in time," Doris squawked at one point. "Jim?"

"Yes, my dear?"

"Why did the ancient Greeks leave them so *unfinished*?"

"What do you mean?"

"Well, they're all so exquisitely beautiful, true to life in every detail, so accurate in all their forms, but – raark – they're all so colourless!"

"Ah. They weren't always like this, you know."

"Oh?"

"Quaaoo?"

"No, they were originally painted, from head to toe, wing to talon, in perfect colours of nature, and with bright and arresting tones in their clothing. The ancient Greeks thought that to leave them as bare white marble was to leave them incomplete, as though the sculpture were only half done. Look." Jim slowed his pace and led Doris and Brenda to a corner of the Gallery through which they were passing.

He stood before a stele, or tablet, of marble that was about as big as his torso. "This is very famous. It's the gravestone of the sailor Demokleides. See, that's him, carved up there on top of that wave. He's looking out to sea, as though he's yearning for his lost life. Now if you look very carefully at the area of marble below the water-line of the wave, you might see what I mean."

Doris blinked, squinting her small dark eyes. Brenda fluttered her eyelashes and squinted her large unfathomable ones.

"Rerk," squawked Doris. "There're traces of blue. Look, Brenda!"

Brenda gave a yes-you-noisy-bird-I-can-see-it snort.

"Here," said Jim, "they coloured the bitter waves like that to add the depth of sorrow to—"

"Please, Cairo Jim!" Euripides's voice echoed and bounced urgently off the walls and motionless exhibits. "The scene of the crime is this way."

Jim nodded and once again they followed the Keeper.

By the time they arrived at the corner before the Gallery of Forgotten Gods, the immense coolness inside the Museum had dried Jim's shirt, Doris's feathers and Brenda's many hairy places. With an abruptness that set his pile of curls quivering, Euripides stopped and held up his hand. "We are about to turn into the Gallery of Forgotten Gods," he announced solemnly. "If you have known sorrow before today, it will be nothing to what lays ahead."

Doris fluttered from Jim's shoulder to Brenda's fore hump, and Euripides ushered them all around the corner, into the Gallery, where they found themselves standing before the great glass and mahogany display case. The air in here was heavy enough to be sliced through with a dagger.

"Here, my friends." Doodah's voice was small, wounded, astounded, without hope. "This is where the Sacred Alabastron of Cronus has been housed for the last eighty years or so. Now, she has piffled it."

They all looked at him quizzically. "I mean, *pilfered*."

"She?" asked Cairo Jim.

"That no-good, thieving scoundreless! That dishonest, multi-faced—"

"You mean to say you know who did it?"

"I have my suspicions." Fury ran through Euripides's eyes, lighting them up like flames.

"Who was it?"

"Doctor Hermione Dinkus!"

"Hermione Dinkus!" gasped Jim, and Doris gave an incredulous squawk. "But that's impossible."

"You know her, of course, Cairo Jim. You are both members of the same revered Society, are you not?"

"That we surely are. I've been what you might call an indirect acquaintance of hers for quite a few years." The archaeologist-poet ran his thumbnail around his grim lips. "Are you *sure* it was Hermione Dinkus who did this dreadful thing?"

"As sure as Sarpedon died like a pincushion in ancient battle."

"Please, Mr Doodah—"

"Euripides."

"Please, Euripides, tell us what happened here. Everything, as accurately as you can recount. It's all so strange that a woman like Hermione Dinkus would stoop to such a thing."

For the next five minutes, Euripides recounted the incidents that had taken place on the day of disaster. He started in a low voice, but as he progressed, his voice got higher and his eyes widened. By the time he came to the bit about Hermione Dinkus's dizzy spell and her request for a glass of water, his indignation and sense of outrage had risen so much they were almost spurting through his curls.

"...so, naturally, I went to fetch her the water. She is such a – if you'll forgive the expression – *monumentally built* woman that I felt it was the only thing to do. Why, if she fell, there could have been all kinds of damage done to the floor."

"Monumentally built?" interrupted Jim.

"Oh, I am *so* sorry, you didn't forgive the expression. I don't normally let myself be so descriptive about women, but under the circumstances—"

"No, no, it's not that. It's just that I'd hardly use *that* description for Hermione Dinkus. Would you, Doris?"

The macaw opened her huge wings and closed them around herself again. "It'd be like saying your pinkie finger was Mr Universe," she said, perplexed.

"Exactly," Jim nodded. "The only monumental thing about her is the way that she's a pillar of honesty and decency."

Euripides frowned. "I do not understand."

"Doctor Hermione Dinkus, at least the Doctor Hermione Dinkus whom we know, is a very tiny, very fragile woman. She must be ninety years old at least. Even if she fell onto a floor of marshmallow, she wouldn't make a dent in it."

"She was blown 'from the organ-pipe of frailty'," Doris crowed, quoting a snatch from *King John*.

"And besides," Jim went on, "we only recently saw her at the Old Relics Society, at a special clog-dancing theme evening. She wasn't dancing herself, of course – it's a bit hard when you're confined to a wheelchair – but she was slapping her leg-brace most enthusiastically in time to the music. It was during a quiet lull on that night that she intimated to us that her travelling days were over."

The Keeper of the Gallery of Forgotten Gods blinked, and his rounded face instantaneously drained of all its colour.

Jim reached out and put his hand on the shaken man's shoulder. "I'm afraid you might not only have been robbed, Euripides, but also *hoodwinked* by an impostor."

"But who? Who would be devious enough to masquerade in such a way?"

At this point, Doris whispered something into Brenda's ear, and the Wonder Camel (with Doris aboard) lumbered quietly over to the great glass and mahogany display case by the far wall.

"Tell me everything you can remember about her," Jim said, leading Euripides to a low wooden bench at the side of the Gallery. Here they sat and Euripides had a good scratch of his right kneecap, an action which often helped him to think. "Was there anything she had with her that appeared suspicious? Anything that might have helped her to perpetrate the shameful act, for example?"

"Let me think ... on the top of my head—"

Jim quickly looked up at the small pile of curls.

"—I would say not. Oh! Wait a moment. There was something strange."

"Yes?" Jim leaned closer. "What?"

"She carried a bag, black it was, a Glumstone."

Jim looked at him quizzically.

"I mean, a *Gladstone*. She was most particular about this bag, wouldn't let it out of her grasp for more than a few seconds. At one stage, out on the front steps of the Museum, I recall that she put it down. When I was about to escort her inside, I picked up the bag, and you should have witnessed the fuss!"

"Fuss?"

"She came at me like a sweaty, perfumed, yashmaked *lorry*, Cairo Jim, oh my goodness yes, and *snatched* it back. It is a wonder that I still have my arms remaining in their sockets!"

"She wore a yashmak?"

"She did." Euripides screwed up his nose. "An appalling colour, you should have seen it. A watery yellow that did not go at all well with her enormous mauve frock. I should have smelled a rodent then and there. The fashion was quite repulsive."

The archaeologist-poet made a small grimace.

"But what I wanted to tell you about that bag," continued Euripides, "was this: it has only just come back to me now. In the few seconds I had that bag in my hand, I was acutely aware of *something moving around inside it*. Scrabbling around, as though it was moving very fast, fiercely even."

"Oh, for the love of Rameses," muttered Jim. He rested his chin in his cupped hand and began to add up all the physical characteristics that Euripides had detailed so far. Jim didn't like the picture that was emerging in his imagination.

At that moment Doris gave a sharp, excited screech at the other end of the Gallery. "Reeeerrraaarrrk! Look, come over here!"

The two men sprang up and went to join the macaw and Wonder Camel. Doris hopped onto Jim's shoulder and pointed with her wing to a hole, perfectly round and about fifteen centimetres in diameter, that had been cut into the glass.

"Gracious," Jim whispered.

"That was how she pinched the Sacred Alabastron of Cronus," said Euripides. "See? The hole is only a fraction bigger than a hand's width. She just whipped in her hand and snatched out the alabastron. She was most quick."

"This glass must've been cut with a diamond drill. It's so clean." Jim looked at Euripides. "How long were you away from the Gallery?"

"I can't have been more than two minutes. I was speedy."

"Raark! It'd take more than two minutes to cut this hole with a diamond drill," squawked Doris. "No, this hole was made with something very different. Something just as *natural* as a diamond, but much more dangerous…"

"What, Doris?"

"Only one thing on the planet could have made this clean cut so quickly: a bird's beak." She paused and blinked sternly.

"Go on, my dear."

"Not any old bird's beak, oh, no siree. Only the razor-sharp, extra-strong mandible of a particular species of bird could have done this. Only the beak of a—"

"QUAAAOOOO!"

Brenda, who had been inspecting the other relics and artefacts housed behind the glass, had found something of interest.

"It seems that Brenda has found something of interest," commented Euripides, who was catching on quickly.

Jim reached over and gently stroked the Wonder Camel's snout. "What, my lovely?"

Brenda rotated her big head, and her snout came to point at something to the right of the hole – a small lekythos vase, no bigger than ten centimetres high. It was painted with a touching scene showing two women holding flowers and bowls, and looking most sombre.

 49

"Ah," Euripides said. "That was found many years ago at a site in the west of Greece, where the Great Gods were once worshipped."

Doris jumped and fluttered from Jim's shoulder and onto the top of Brenda's head, coming to rest between her ears, on her mane. "Rark! Listen to what the display card under it says." She cleared her throat, blinked twice, and read in her best and fruitiest parrot tones:

"A woman and a maid bearing offerings with which to decorate a grave-monument. The inscription reads: *'Kromippos, the son of Kromokleides, is handsome'*."

There were several seconds of silence, and then everyone looked at Brenda. "So, Brenda?" asked Doris. "What's so special about that?"

Brenda gave a mini-snort and lifted her head sharply, causing Doris to flutter unexpectedly into the air. Then the Wonder Camel rotated her head again, but froze the movement in the middle of the action, so that her head was held at a very strange angle to her neck.

"I think she's seen something on the underside of the lekythos," Jim said. He, too, bent his neck so that he could peer at the vase at a point where the body of it met the bottom rim. "Well, swoggle me sculpturally," he muttered.

"Rerk!" Doris turned her head to the strange position, and so did Euripides Doodah. "What is it, Jim?"

"There's something written there. Very finely, as though it's been done with the tip of a pin. It's quite hard to read with the naked eye, though. Just a moment."

He reached over to his knapsack, which hung from

one of the side fasteners on Brenda's saddle. Delving in, he quickly extricated his "Perspicacious"-brand archaeological magnifying glass with the brown leather handle and the never-in-your-lifetime-will-it-crack shatterproof glass. This he held to his eye as he returned his head to the unnatural angle.

"Hmm. Goodness, it's still difficult to read, even with my 'Perspicacious' brand archaeological magnifying glass."

"Look carefully, please, Cairo Jim." Euripides Doodah was shifting from foot to foot impatiently and, with the way his head was turned, he looked in danger of snapping something he would rather not. "I am sure those markings are freshly made!"

Jim squinted, and moved the magnifying glass away from his eye, closer to the glass in the display case, and then back to his eye again. Slowly, as though a mist was clearing before him, the small pin-like pricks on the ancient lekythos began to join up, moving together until they were becoming readable words.

"There," Jim murmured, "I can just about make it out now. Right there, underneath where it says *Kromippos, the son of Kromokleides, is handsome*', there's something been added."

"Rark, what?"

"Oh, what?"

"Quaaoo? Quaaoo?"

Cairo Jim saw the words slowly, one after the other. "'But not as handsome as...'" He broke off and

straightened his head, lowering the magnifying glass to his side with a dreadful hollowness in his arm.

"But not as handsome as *who*?" spluttered Doris.

The dreadful hollowness spread up his arm, through his shoulderblades, down into his chest and legs until it arrived with a hurtling rudeness into his poetry cavity. He turned to face his colleagues, and his voice gave utterance to his worst fears:

No matter what the weather, or where the
upturned stone,
or if we go together, or if we roam alone,
where ere the seeds of History are scattered or
are sown,
SO TOO WE'LL FIND THE VILLAINY OF—

5

A VAGABOND GENIUS

CAPTAIN NEPTUNE BONE, that much-disgraced archaeologist and most unfinancial member of the Old Relics Society, was sitting lazily on an inflatable, velvet-clad comfy chair next to his rented Bugatti automobile. A long, fat, stinking cigar was clenched between his fleshy lips, its grey-green smoke curling upwards and sideways into his neatly clipped moustache and beard. On top of his basketball-like head there perched a fez from his vast collection – this model was of a mustard tint, and had a shiny, burgundy-coloured tassel hanging limply down the back.

The large man was enjoying the shade of the sprawling olive tree under which he was relaxing. He was enjoying even more one of his most important indulgences: with careful and fussy strokes, he was sawing away with his manicure file at his beloved fingernails. As he savoured the feeling of the file and the smell of the cigar and the refreshing temperature of the shade, and as he gloated at the memory of the act he had recently perpetrated, a song began to emerge from his throat and was carried aloft by the gentle breeze that played around him:

Mine is a Vagabond Genius,
a brilliance quite misunderstood.
I'm but a square peg in this world of round dregs,
where honours are saved for the good...

Mine's *just* a Vagabond Genius,
a cleverness all overlooked.
A life of dismissal, an unblown great whistle,
as yet un-journalled and un-booked...

Mine's *BUT* a Vagabond Genius,
my talents are always ignored,
my wondrous great vision subject to derision,
dismissed by the bland and the bored...

But quite soon the world, with its banners unfurled,
will hear the full tell of my story.
And then – oh and how! – every kneecap shall bow
to the light of my own subtle glory...

"CRAAARRRK!" The rocket-like squawk of his companion, the raven known to the world as Desdemona, interrupted Bone's musicality. He sighed loudly and took a long drag on the cigar.

"These walls do not a prison make!" crowed the bird, who was sitting on the ground near Bone's feet, with his black Gladstone bag by her flea-infested side. She peered through her slitted red eyes at the manicuring sight above her. "That was the last time you ever shove me in a handbag, you great fashion victim, you!"

"Oh, really?" Bone sneered. He blew a strong pillar of smoke at her. "What makes you so absolutely certain of that, you odious ornithological oddity?"

"*This*," spat the raven. She lowered her head and opened her razor-sharp beak. Then, in a fierce and ferocious frenzy, she hacked and tore away at the bag, spitting bits of the tattered leather over her shoulder and into the air, until all that was left was a pathetic wire skeleton. The whole demolition process took no more than ten seconds. "Nevermore, nevermore, nevermore!" sang the bird. "Ha ha ha ha ha ha!"

"Arrrr," said Neptune Bone, his lip curling into a scowl. He crossed his legs (it was a delicate manoeuvre, as he was very plump in the thigh department) and smoothed down the chequered fabric of his plus-fours trousers so that there would be minimal creasing around the kneecap area. "That was a good and useful bag, you smelly, useless bag."

"I don't care if it belonged to the King of Persia. I'm never getting into one of those things again. I came over all clutterophobic in there." Her eyeballs throbbed painfully at the memory.

"It was necessary for our deception, fester-feathers. I had to find some way of secreting you. Think about it. If I'd just waltzed up to the Museum with you on my *arm*, that silly little Doodah man would have taken one look and run the marathon to Marathon. You tend to have that sort of effect on human beings, you know."

"Human beings? Hah! What do I care about human beings?"

"*I* am a human being, Desdemona. A Sheer and Utter Genius, *I* admit it, but a human being nevertheless. And it is I upon whom you are dependent for your freedom."

Desdemona lifted her black-as-pitch wing and waved it dismissively at him. "Oh, yeah?"

"You bet your barbules. You know as well as I, if it weren't for me you'd be in the hands of the Antiquities Squad by now. How long have they been after you since that little incident with the appendage you hacked off the Sapiential Sphinx of Saqqara?"

"How long have they been after you since you sold accommodation in the Great Pyramid of Khufu to that busload of French tourists?"

"Hrmph, never mind about that. Anyway, you weren't the only one who had to go through an unnatural experience to get the Sacred Alabastron of Cronus. Do you think I actually *delighted* in having to put on women's clothing?"

She raised a flea-riddled eyebrow at him.

"*Of course I didn't*, you rude rodent with wings." He buffed his fingernails briskly. "Although the yashmak was altogether different from how I thought it would be … much more natural and flowing, if you really want to know."

"I don't," rasped the raven. "I couldn't care less if you decided to wear one for the rest of your life. Although I'd be your biggest supporter if you decided instead to wear one of those headbags with little eye-holes in it and no opening for the mouth. That'd be a vast improvement…"

Bone shot her a filthy glare. "Don't be so rude, you fleaball."

"Well, what do you expect?" she spat. "You drag me all the way over here and then stuff me into a handbag and make me use my highly sensitive choppers to cut through plate glass … yeerrgh, I'm still coughing up little slivers all over the place. Do you expect me to be *grateful*?"

"Of course I do."

Desdemona looked at him sideways, and the feathers down her spine hackled. "You've been wearing those fezzes for too long, you know. They don't give you enough protection from the sun. I think, Captain Neptune Flannelbottom Bone, that you've finally lost what distorted and little reasoning power you ever had."

"Arrr," murmured the large man. He replaced the file in his manicure case and gently shut it. Then he withdrew his cigar from his lips, smiled flabbily at the bird, and quickly ashed the cigar on her forehead.

"Aaaahaaahaaaa!" moaned Desdemona, who enjoyed such acts – they helped keep down her flea population.

"Oh, no, my dear Desdemona, I have my full collection of faculties. All of my brilliance has gone undiminished. In fact, very soon, I will be even more brilliant than now. Greater than I presently am. More powerful to boot."

"What?" she rasped in her whatever-are-you-ranting-about-now? voice.

"Oh, yes indeed. Magnificently more powerful." He stood and looked out towards the hazy horizon, which lay eastwards across the enormous grove of olive trees before him. "In fact, I will be more powerful, more important, altogether more potent than any other *human being* in this world."

Desdemona shuddered; she had never heard him use that tone when he had said the words "human being" before. It was as though, through his intonation, he had screwed up the words and hurled them over a cliff.

"Yes," he continued, "thanks to that small but significant alabastron, I shall become what I've always deserved to become."

"What's that? Slimmer?"

"Shut your beak! I'd take a swipe at you if you were not beneath my contempt. No, you wretched, whining weirdo, I shall become something that you could not possibly hope to comprehend."

"Go on," said Desdemona, stretching out on her belly and resting her elbowfeathers on the grass in front of her. She cupped her head on the endfeathers of her wings and waggled her talons in the air. "Tell me more. I'm *dying* to hear how a stupid little vase can make you *great*."

Bone held out his hand and ashed his cigar into her eyes. "All right then, gormless. If you really want to know, I'll tell you. Although not everything."

"Why not? I'm your companion, aren't I?"

"Regrettably, you are, but that doesn't mean I have to spill all of the beans just yet. No, I'll tell you a tad, and you must be content with that. As for the rest, time will reveal all."

Desdemona rolled her red eyeballs. She had heard him spout this – one of his favourite sayings – a thousand times. "Go on then," she said scornfully (but with well-disguised curiosity), "tell me a *tad.*"

He reached into his emerald-green waistcoat and, from an interior pocket, withdrew a sheet of neatly folded paper. This he held before him, his eyes sleering across it as though it was a cheque for a billion dollars. He took a deep suck on his cigar and exhaled the smoke in a nasty plume.

"Let me tell you a little something about History, Desdemona. A little something that may help you understand why we're here in Greece." He cleared his throat and began to speak in a low rumble, his voice rich and quietly excited. "History, as I have come to discover, is a saga of disposability. Everything grows old, everything has to change. And throughout this great sweeping procession we have come to label as 'History', it has frequently happened that when something has grown old, when it is time for that something to be changed, then that something has often been discarded. Tossed aside. Disposed of. Or *put into a sunless, darkened place, never to be remembered.* Like baby and the bathwater, thrown out the window."

"What?" croaked the raven. "Who threw baby and the bathwater out the window? What malevolence! Not even *I'd*—"

"Shut up, you flapdoodler, it's only an expression."

"Crark!" Desdemona pecked a munching flea from off her wing and chewed it thoughtfully.

"As I was saying, History and disposability have long been intertwined." He curled one fleshy finger around another. "And so it is that History leads us down the Path of Forgetfulness, along which many things are disposed of. And, as times change, as the world grows a little older – decade by decade, century by century, millennium by millennium – that Path of Forgetfulness becomes astonishingly wide. More like a superhighway, if you can picture it. And along this colossally wide superhighway, there is much that has been forgotten. More than you could ever begin to dream about."

"Like what?"

Bone sucked on the cigar and turned the piece of paper over in his fingers. When he exhaled, a smile appeared on his lips. "Like all manner of things. The beliefs that men and women held. The buildings that men and women built. The stories they told, and the songs they sang. The perfumes and the clothing they wore. Even – and here, his beard and moustache bristled, and Desdemona thought she could see his fez tassel moving gently back and forth upon the fez – "even the gods they worshipped. It is dreadful indeed, when these things fall by the Path. It is, my wretched fiend, a tragedy, and most unforgivable."

He began to pace up and down, smoking all the while. His rate of sucking and exhaling increased the more he talked. (If somebody had viewed him from a distance, they might have mistaken him for a steam-driven locomotive engine.)

"But occasionally, a Genius such as what I am finds his way down this glorious Path. And when that happens, my dear Desdemona, there is much to be reaped. That stupid little vase, as you so delicately described it, that Sacred Alabastron of Cronus which we have packed carefully away in the Bugatti, contains something that was disposed of a long, long while ago. Once upon a time – oh, I used to hate those words, but not any more – *once upon a time*, a new order came along, you see, a new order that was quite different to the order of things as they had been standing. Now, in order for this new order to have some order and to become established, the leaders of the new order decided to get rid of the old order. That way their new order could go ahead, without interruption, or riots, or other messy disturbances. Things changed, as they do throughout History. This is why we have been led to the alabastron. That little piece of pottery holds the key to *how* things changed. With it, we are going to change things back."

"Crark, I don't get it. How can one pottery vase—?"

"That's enough of that particular tad of my Master Plan for the time being. I don't want to tell you too much more now in case we become separated. Much as I like the idea of *that* concept, I'm afraid you're needed for the time being."

"What's that bit of paper you're waving around?"

"This will help us set things right. I tore it out of a volume I found in the library of the Archaeological

Museum, in the week before we became Dinkus and Gladstone. History causes people to forget, and, in this particular instance, that is a blessing for us. You see, most people in this world – archaeologists and antiquarians included – have completely forgotten what the Sacred Alabastron of Cronus stands for. They have no idea, any more, about the new order and the old order."

"I bet you didn't, either, until you found that book."

"That's neither here nor there. The alabastron was just sitting in that display case in the Museum, gathering dust, being viewed by maybe half a dozen people in a single year. To them it would have been merely another vase in that huge and echoing place, along with the thousands of other vases in the hundreds of other display cases. But for us, Desdemona, thanks to my Utter Genius and great breadth of vision, that alabastron and these instructions" – he waved the folded paper in the air – "are going to change the course of the here-and-now so that … oh, let me catch my breath at the prospect of it all … so that *History will be the pearl in my very own private oyster*! ARRRRRRRRRR!"

The raven lay there, looking at him. She had been with Neptune Bone through many schemes, had accompanied him to foreign lands in pursuit of seemingly absurd prizes and ambitious plunder. Many was the time that she had thought he was teetering on the edge of some sort of egomaniacal oblivion. But today, as she listened to him raving, she knew he was up to something particularly ambitious.

"What do you mean, Captain? What exactly are you after? Will you get lots of gold, like in the Red Sea after you dived for Sekheret? Or maybe some kind of potion that can do flabbergasting things, like the one you went looking for at ChaCha Muchos, in Peru?"★

"Oh, I will get much more than any of those things put together. I will get what no man before me has ever been able to achieve ... a universal power the likes of which could not fill even your hugest dreams! Hahahahahahaaaarrrr!"

All at once he stopped his hysterical gurgling. He threw his cigar to the ground and pulled out his gold fob-watch from the pocket of his waistcoat. "Hmm. It's getting late. I've wasted enough time gabbling here with you. Come, we have a great distance to cover before nightfall."

"What? Where are we off to now?"

"North, to Delphi."

"Why?"

Bone put away his fob-watch and carefully unfolded the torn-out page. "Because, you inquisitive ignoramus, according to this, there are several items I need to collect before we can go to the final ancient site to perform the Divine Opening Ceremony. The Museum at Delphi has such an item." He silently read some of the words printed on the page, and then re-folded it and

---

★ See *Cairo Jim and the Sunken Sarcophagus of Sekheret* and *Cairo Jim on the Trail to ChaCha Muchos*

put it in the backside pocket of his plus-fours. "Arr. Yes, we have a little pilfering to do. Although I prefer to think of it as picking up a few necessary little items. Sort of like going to the supermarket, really." With a sturdy, bold (and wobbling) stride he made for the Bugatti.

"Crark, wait for me." Desdemona flew after him. "I think I've heard of this Delphi joint. Isn't that where they once had a big monocle that used to tell the answers to riddles? You know, the monocle of Delphi?"

Bone opened the door of the automobile and squeezed himself onto the soft leather seat. "That was the *Oracle* of Delphi, you moron. If you had a brain under those feathers, I think I'd be alarmed." He slipped on his driving gloves to protect his precious fingernails, and pressed the starter button.

"And if you had an alarm under that fez, I'd be— Hey, wait for me! Creerraarrrrkk!"

With a mighty flapping of her wings, she spiralled off after the dust-clouded Bugatti as it bumped away through the olive-tree forest.

6

IMAGINING IT THROUGH

"WHERE ON EARTH has Euripides got to? He's been gone for ages, Jim, and we're stuck here, in this Gallery, waiting for him. Rark! We should be out there, trying to find this alabastron. By my feathers, if it's in Bone's pudgy hands, he's probably flogging it off to some wealthy and devious antiquities collector even as we squawk, speak and snort! Why can't we just go out and start looking, Jim?"

"Steady on, my dear." Cairo Jim reached out and patted down Doris's exasperated crest. "Don't get yourself in a flap."

"Quaaooo," snorted Brenda, who thought that was witty.

"It wouldn't be much good looking for something when we don't know exactly what it looks like, would it?"

"*I* know exactly what it looks like," Doris spluttered, opening her wings and closing them quickly. "It's tall, fat, badly attired and wears a fez of clashing colours on its chubby head."

"No, not Bone, I meant the alabastron. That's why Euripides has gone to get that book he told us about. He says it contains the best photograph of the alabastron, one that shows all the decorations on it. If we know exactly what's painted on the alabastron, we'll

 65

be able to identify it properly when we find it."

Doris fluttered from the bench, where she had been sitting next to Jim, and rose into the air in the middle of the Gallery of Forgotten Gods. Here she swooped up and down anxiously. "Hmph. If he takes any longer, my feathers'll turn grey, and I'll get wrinkles all around my—"

At that moment, the sound of echoing footsteps rose and filled the Gallery. A few seconds later, Euripides Doodah emerged from around the corner, carrying a thick, leather-bound volume in one hand and a large cup of hot, steaming coffee in the other.

"Oh, I surely need this," he said breathily, "it is like a life-giving elixir to me. The marshmallows floating in the top soon dissolve and give the coffee a very interesting flavour, not to mention a kick to the taste-buds."

"Have you been drinking marshmallowed coffee for long?" asked Jim.

"Oh, for years. At first I always used to get the most dreadful headaches, though, here, behind my left eye. Every time I had taken the first sip of a cup of marshmallowed coffee, my left eye would *blaze* with pain. I could barely see through it. I'd thought the combination of coffee and marshmallow was somehow responsible, but soon I discovered the *real* reason."

"Oh, yes?"

"Yes. I kept forgetting to take the teaspoon out of the cup before I started drinking." He sat down on the bench next to Jim. "Are you sure I cannot get all of you some little refreshment?"

"No, thank you," answered the archaeologist-poet. "We'd much rather see this photograph."

"Oh, yes, yes, of course. It's right in here."

Brenda, who had been sitting cross-legged in the corner, rose silently and lumbered over to the bench. Doris swooped down and perched on Jim's shoulder.

"This book," said Euripides as he turned the pages, "was written over fifty years ago by Professor Helena Hattbocks, an obscure historian with a passion for the old gods. It's not a very reliable source, as far as the words go – I am afraid that old Helena tended to get a little towed off by her imagination when it came to legends … er, I mean *carried away* by her imagination – but the photographs and illustrations are most excellent. Ah, here we are."

He opened the volume completely flat and laid it upon his knees, so that everyone could have an unobscured view of the black-and-white photograph. For several seconds they all beheld it in silence.

It was the traditional shape for an alabastron – slender, with a round base, and a small lip at the top. Underneath this lip protruded two tiny, semicircular discs, which would have served as handles for the vessel. Beneath the photograph was a small caption: "*The Sacred Alabastron of Cronus. Age unknown, but probably dates back to 3,000 BC. Height: sixteen centimetres.*"

Doris made a small cooing noise. "It's quite beautiful, eh, Jim?" she whispered close to Jim's ear.

Indeed it was. The photograph showed clearly the

decorations on the front of the alabastron. At the top, just under the lip, was painted a billowing scene of the heavens. Wild and towering blue and grey clouds appeared to be swelling in from one side, obliterating the sunlight. Below, a series of figures – they looked to Cairo Jim like giants – seemed to be cowering, to be shrinking away from the turbulence and uncertainty above.

"Quaaooo!" Brenda flared her nostrils and motioned with her eyelashes to something in the cloudscape.

"Look," said Jim, "Brenda's found something."

Doris blinked. "Rark. There's something coming down from the clouds."

"So there is." Jim peered intently at whatever it was that was coming down from the clouds.

"Ah," said Euripides. "That would probably be the first of the Great Gods."

Jim looked at him. "The Great Gods?"

Euripides nodded. "Maybe even Zeus himself."

"Tell us more. What story does the scene depict?"

Euripides took a long sip of his coffee. "It is only a legend, Cairo Jim. Nothing but that. It has nothing really to do with the alabastron."

"Legend or no legend, I'd like to hear it. It may cast some light on why Bone took it. He's evil, there's no doubt about that, Euripides, but he's also *clever*. Extremely clever. He's one of the most resourceful men I've ever had the misfortune to come across."

Euripides sighed. "I do not go in for following such

legends myself. They have no real place in my profession. Give me facts, I say. Unfortunately, the Governors of the Museum think differently. They believe in all of this imaginary nonsense."

"It may not be imaginary nonsense," said Jim. "What significance do the Great Gods have regarding this alabastron?"

Euripides Doodah took another sip of his coffee and then patted the page facing the photograph. "You can read it for yourself, right here. Old Helena Hattbocks was certainly one for the fantastic."

Jim looked eagerly down at the page and read aloud. "'Chapter Nineteen: The Sacred Alabastron of Cronus. Or, Gods But Not Forgotten'."

Doris squawked noisily, and everyone jumped. "Reeraark! I can feel it in my plumes – we may be onto something. This could be why that scoundrel wanted it! Read on, Jim." She moved her head and neck impatiently up and down.

Euripides rolled his eyes, but in a polite manner, as befitted his gentlemanly nature. "Please, be my gust."

Jim looked at him quizzically.

"I mean, *guest*." He slid the volume across into Jim's lap.

The archaeologist-poet cleared his throat and began to read in his quiet, steady tone:

"The Sacred Alabastron of Cronus is a small example of artwork from the early Archaic period.

The artefact was discovered in 1876, in the ruins of a temple dedicated to Poseidon on the island of Samothraki. The alabastron is traditionally regarded as the simplest of all ancient Greek vases; the Sacred Alabastron of Cronus is not a particularly breathtaking example of either the ancient potter's or the ancient artist's craft, but is pleasingly decorated. It is most interesting, however, for its depiction of the climactic battle that raged for twenty years between the Titans and the Great Gods, a brief description of which is set out here."

"The Titans?" asked Doris. "Who were the Titans?"

"Sh, my dear, I'm sure Helena Hattbocks will tell us."

The hairs in Brenda's mane bristled and stood on end as she prepared herself for the legend.

Jim continued reading:

"Nobody knows for certain when the old gods were done away with, but because of the survival of the Sacred Alabastron of Cronus, we do know *how* they were done away with. These old gods were known as the Titans, and there were six of them: Oceanus, Coeus, Crius, Hyperion, Iapetus and Cronus. Oceanus was the eldest and Cronus the youngest. The Titans had six sisters, or Titanesses: Theia, Rhea, Themis, Mnemosyne,

Phoebe and Tethys. Of all the Titans and Titanesses, our main interest lies with Cronus, for it was he who was responsible for setting the fates in motion which eventually made it possible for the Olympians, led by Zeus, to overtake the Titans.

"All of the other Titans went off to do one thing or another: fight wars or make new oceans or practise handicrafts. Cronus was left by himself to reign over the world as it was beginning to form. Being by himself, he soon became lonely and so, with the aid of Rhea, he had three daughters – Hestia, Demeter and Hera – and three sons – Hades, Poseidon and Zeus."

"So that's where they came from," blinked Doris.
"According to the legends," sighed Euripides.
Jim continued reading:

"But there was something terrible waiting to happen: Cronus had been cursed because of his action of turning his father, Uranus, off the throne. Cronus's mother, Gaea, prophesised that Cronus, like his father, would be dethroned by his own children. To prevent this threat from coming true, Cronus ate whole the first five of his children.

"The sixth child, Zeus, was saved, thanks to the quick thinking of Rhea. She wrapped a bundle of rocks in Zeus's swaddling clothes, and fed those to her brother. Cronus devoured them, believing them to be the infant. Rhea and Gaea then whisked Zeus away and hid him in a cave on Crete.

"And so the years passed. Cronus continued to reign over the world, and formed many strange relationships with groups of nature-spirits, which abounded in the northern islands of Greece. (And which many people believe still do.) Meanwhile, Zeus grew up in his Cretan cave, where he was nursed by Amalthea, a good-natured nymph. He grew strong and practised athletics and various shield and spear activities with the Young Men – or Curetes – who lived on the island. The Curetes performed unceasing war dances while Zeus grew up, and it is believed that this loud and never-ending activity imbued Zeus with many of his warrior qualities. It is also believed that through the company of the Young Men, Zeus discovered his powers and his divine calling.

"Finally, the time came for Zeus to fulfil Gaea's prophecy. He returned to Cronus's regions and met up with one of Oceanus's daughters, who was named Metis. Metis gave Zeus a potion, which he slipped into Cronus's wine when Cronus was not looking. Cronus became horribly ill, and vomited up all of his eaten children, who were still alive inside his belly."

Jim screwed up his nose.

"Out they all came and immediately joined forces with Zeus. It was the beginning of the end for the Titans."

Here he paused, and read silently ahead a little. "Well, I'll be swoggled," he murmured.

"What? Go on, Jim." Doris's head and neck were moving up and down as if they were on a spring.

"My goodness!"

"Quaaooo!" Brenda stomped a hoof firmly on the marble floor.

The archaeologist-poet shook his head slowly, as though the action might help him to comprehend the information he had just silently read. "Listen to this," he whispered:

"After twenty years of massive warfare, Zeus emerged victorious. He bound up all of the remaining Titans – Cronus included – and imprisoned them forever in a small alabastron, the stopper of which was never to be removed."

He turned sharply to Euripides. "The Sacred Alabastron of Cronus, did it have any kind of stopper in it?"

Doodah frowned and had a scratch of his right kneecap. "Let me think … ah, yes, I do believe it did.

Mmm, I remember now. The last time I dusted it – a few months ago, it was – I tried to take out the stopper to get the dust away from the inside rim. It wouldn't budge."

"Thank Hera for that," said Cairo Jim.

"You are not suggesting that the Sacred Alabastron of Cronus—?"

Doris flapped her wings. "Hey, hang on to your llamas, Jim," she squawked. "You don't think—?"

"I do indeed," answered Jim. "Neptune Bone has swiped an entire ancient order of supernatural powers, all in the one little vase!"

"If you'll forgive me for saying so, Cairo Jim, that is preposterous." Euripides stood and began walking anxiously around his Gallery. "What you have just read is a legend, nothing more and nothing less. It has nothing to do with History. You should be out there right now, looking for this Bone rapscallion, and trying to obtain repossession of the alabastron. All of that" – he pointed at the book in Jim's lap – "is nothing more than a product of people's imaginations! And, if you'll forgive me, I think *your* imagination is galloping away with you."

Jim's eyes were grim, but a tiny smile lifted the corners of his lips. "Maybe it is, maybe you're right, but being a poet, I find that my imagination is a most valuable asset, Euripides. And many's the time when a little bit of imagination has greatly assisted me in our archaeological discoveries."

"Rark," chipped in Doris. "That's for sure. Never underestimate the old imagination. 'Look how imagination blows him', as Mr Shakespeare wrote in *Twelfth Night*."

"And I'll be blowed, too," thought Brenda with a snort. "If it means going along with Jim."

Jim smiled fully now. "Maybe we need to imagine this whole thing through ... only that way can we begin to comprehend exactly what Bone is planning."

"Hmm." Euripides stopped pacing and clasped his hands behind his back. "Well, I still think that this is all a fairy tale. Nothing more."

"Does it say anything more that we might need to know?" Doris asked.

"Let's see." Jim returned his attention to the place at which he'd finished reading. His heart almost stopped.

"Cairo Jim, are you all right?" Euripides came over to him and Doris and Brenda. "The colour just drained straight from your cheeks!"

"Give him air, give him air!" Doris flapped her wings in front of her friend's face.

"You look like you have seen a ghost from the Underworld," said Euripides.

"Listen to this," Jim gasped. He gripped the book in shaking hands as he read:

"If the stopper of the alabastron is ever taken out, the original Titans will return to the present-day world. Whoever is responsible for the removal of the stopper will be rewarded by the Titans with the utmost prize: immediate deification."

Cairo Jim looked up and, for the first time in a long time, there was real fear in his eyes. With a quavering, dreadful voice, he spoke: "*Neptune Bone plans to become a god!*"

Doris gave a screech, a long, drawn-out scraping of sound that echoed mightily around the Museum's tranquil and human-less galleries, as though one of the Titans himself had dragged his gigantic fingernails down the divine blackboard of the world.

CONVINCING EURIPIDES

"WE'VE NOT A SECOND, not a speck, not an *inkling* of time to waste," stressed Cairo Jim, doing his utmost to control the quavering in his voice. "Euripides, you must accompany us. We'll need your knowledge of this country if we're to travel quickly, as well, of course, as your enlightenment in the historical spheres."

Euripides gulped and began to look nervous. "You— you mean that you want me to *leave* the Museum?"

"Of course. We've got to get onto this trail straight away."

"Oh, but I couldn't."

Jim looked at him curiously, as did Doris and Brenda.

"No, I couldn't possibly leave the Gallery of Forgotten Gods. Why, it is my whole life, Cairo Jim, my whole reason for existing. I would be like a fish without its water if I were away from this establishment."

"Rark!" Doris blinked at him. "But surely you leave it every night when you go home? This'll be like that, only more extended."

The Keeper shifted uncomfortably from foot to foot. "Well, to tell you the truth, Miss Doris, I *don't*. I actually don't have a home, not any more. I used to, years ago, but

I found that I spent so much time in here at the Museum, guarding my precious pieces ... I mean, the *Museum's* precious pieces ... during the days, and spending hours and hours during the nights reading in the Museum's Reading and Research Rooms, that I never got to go to my home. It was not worth keeping a home on, when my home actually lay here. And so the Museum Governors allowed me to erect a small bed in a disused store-room behind this Gallery, and I have remained here. This" – he gestured lovingly (but, Brenda sensed, a little *regretfully*) around the Gallery – "is where I truly belong."

Jim looked puzzled. "But, Euripides, how on earth do you keep your knowledge of antiquities up to date? Surely you leave here to attend conferences and to swap information with other Gallery Keepers?"

The curly-haired man shook his head. "No, never. I read lots, that's all. I subscribe to all the antiquities magazines – *Rubble without a Pause*, *Tidbits of Antiquity*, *Dig Me Up!*, *The Petticoat of History*, *International Dustbusters*, *Thoth's Blurter*, *Expose That Grandeur!* They keep me extremely well-informed."

"But what about eating?" asked Jim. "You must have ventured out to have meals, yes?"

"The Museum Governors provide me with a small stove on which I can heat whatever food I need to consume. One of the cleaning staff buys me weekly food rations and my coffee and marshmallows. It is a most adequate arrangement, and one that has proved to be mutually advantageous. The Museum, you see, gets an extra guard, in the form of me, right around the clock. And I get to be constantly surrounded – every moment of every day – by antiquity."

The archaeologist-poet stroked his bottom lip. "Do you mean to say you *never* leave the Museum?"

"That is what I am saying, Cairo Jim. To tell you the truth, the outside world frightens me a little. It is all so … so modern. History is not important to it at all!"

"Great heavens, man, the outside world is *seething* with history. Only you have to give it *time*. That's how it's made."

"I could not possibly make myself venture outside, I am sorry. This is my niche."

Cairo Jim pushed the book off his lap and onto the bench, and stood. He approached Euripides and held him firmly by the shoulders. "Now, listen to me, Euripides Doodah. I respect what you're telling me, and I respect the niche you have carved for yourself, both in this Museum and in the area of scholarly research. But we are facing a crisis, my friend, and I'm not exaggerating when I tell you that it's more than probably the gravest crisis the world has faced in living memory. That man Bone has in his hands, as we speak, the means of becoming the biggest single threat to global civilisation, to world peace, to the continuing survival of the free human existence. If he pulls off what I think he's trying to pull off, he will have power over us all. Over every living thing, every animal, every blade of grass and speck of dust. He will have us bowing before him with such monstrous regularity that our foreheads may as well be permanently stuck to the ground, and our other ends pointed in the air."

Euripides listened with a growing sense of doom.

"Now, whether you believe all of this about the Sacred Alabastron of Cronus or not is not important to me. This, however, is not a time to be thinking of yourself. Think bigger, Euripides Doodah. Think of the world. Think of the planet. Think of … think of all those coffee plantations and marshmallow factories which may soon be under the control of Captain Neptune Flannelbottom Bone. He has an aversion to coffee, you know, and marshmallows give him spots. He'd more than likely raze all those places to the ground, every one of them."

The curls on Euripides Doodah's head quivered in alarm. He looked into the clear blue eyes of Jim of Cairo, then at his beloved Gallery of Forgotten Gods. Then he shut his eyes and, with a great effort, forced himself to speak. "Okay, you win. I shall come with you."

Jim slapped him lightly on the shoulders. "Champion!" he cried, and Doris and Brenda squawked and snorted in a welcoming, good-on-you sort of way.

"Am I dressed for such an outing?" asked Euripides, looking nervously down at his blue suit. Jim stepped back and surveyed the clothing. After two seconds, he reached out and loosened Euripides's tie, which he pulled free and threw over his shoulder, onto the floor. "You are now," he answered.

The Keeper smiled and undid his top button. As he did so, he thought he sensed a kind of rugged bravura creeping up his spine.

"Come on," Doris flapped, "we've wasted enough time here already. The question on my beak is where do we start looking?"

"That's a very good question, Doris." Jim frowned and began to think.

"Maybe," thought Brenda (in her unique Wonder Camel telepathic way), "the book can guide us."

"Maybe," said Euripides, "the book can guide us."

"Fine thinking, Euripides." Jim strode to the bench and took up the tome. "Now, let's see ... ah, yes:

"In order for the Sacred Alabastron to be opened, the elaborate Divine Opening Ceremony must be performed at an ancient temple in the north-east isles. In order for the Divine Opening Ceremony to take place, several important items of antiquity must be assembled together at the temple. Because of the impossibility of assembling all of these items of antiquity in the same place, it is believed that the alabastron will remain sealed for ever."

Jim stopped reading and looked up. "I'd believe that statement, if all of this didn't involve Bone. The trouble is, 'impossibility' is one word that's not in his vocabulary."

"Read on, read on," screeched the macaw.

He returned to the book:

"The first item that must be collected is an altar, decorated simply, with a shallow hollow scooped out in the exact centre. The altar must be carved from a single piece of Naxian marble. It must have three narrow steps at the front, for use by priests. It must be rectangular and have simple fine lines and elegant volutes on the sides as the sole decoration. Such an altar must be—"

And there he stopped and looked up.

"Must be what?" asked Doris.

"I'm afraid it doesn't say anything else," muttered Jim.

"Eh?" Doris rolled her eyes. "Did Helena Hattbocks give up for the day? What do you mean, it doesn't say anything else?"

"It appears that someone's torn out the next page. That's where we would have found the rest."

"Wait!" exclaimed Euripides. He clapped his hands together once, sharply and loudly. "There is such an altar, one that fits that very description! Oh, my goodness, yes. I read about it only last month in one of my antiquity journals, *Rubble Without a Pause*."

"Where is it?" Jim asked urgently.

"On the floor, beneath my bed. That's where I was reading it. It's just out the back, if you'd like to—"

"No, not the journal, the altar!"

"Ah, yes. Let me think. I remember, it was at Delphi."

"Delphi?"

"Rark, Delphi?"

"Quaaoo, Quaaoo?"

"Yes, in the Delphi Museum. A most beautiful place – so I gather from the photographs I have seen of it, although I have never myself been there. I've never even been out of Athens, if you must know."

"A situation," announced Cairo Jim, "that is soon about to change." He took Brenda by the bridle and, inserting his boot into her stirrup, gripped her saddle. "Ups-a-daisy," he grunted, hoisting himself up into the driver's seat.

"Quaaoooo," Brenda snorted, happy that Jim was in her favourite place.

"Come on, Euripides, up you come. There's plenty of room on top for two, if you don't mind riding close to an *archaeologist*." Jim flashed him a friendly smile and extended his hand. "It's a good thing we decided to bring Brenda's double saddle."

"Oh, but … I've never … it's so *high* up there, I'm sure I'd—"

"REEEERRRRAAARRRRRKKKKK!" Doris's screech ricocheted into Euripides's ear and sent the poor man leaping up into the air. Jim grabbed him by the wrist and hauled him onto Brenda's saddle.

"Thank you, my dear."

"All part of the service," nodded the macaw as she came to land on the rear of Brenda's saddle.

Jim quickly put on his pith helmet and special desert

sun-spectacles, and Euripides clung on to him from behind.

"And away we go," he cried, giving Brenda a small nudge with the inside of his boot.

And away they went.

8

THE HORRIBLE AT DELPHI

DUSK WAS SETTLING SLOWLY as the shiny blue Bugatti purred effortlessly along the narrow road that wound along the mountain peaks of Delphi.

The fading of the day had brought little respite from the heat; unlike the light, the temperature had hardly dropped at all. Even the shadows that began to creep down the craggy slopes seemed to be full of hotness – a dark, seething hotness that spread like molten uncertainty.

"Arrr," moaned Neptune Bone, dabbing at the perspiration on his brow with an eau-de-Cologned handkerchief. "What I'd give for a cool breeze right now."

Desdemona, perched steadfastly on the back of the passenger seat, her blood-red eyeballs throbbing and half-shut against the hot breeze that had been constantly assaulting them on their journey all afternoon, moaned as well. "Oooh, what I'd give for an opened can of choice Japanese seaweed. My belly's making noises like a swingtime orchestra tuning up!"

"Forget about your paunch, you ravenous rebarbativity.* More important things lie in store."

---

* Gunkbucket

 85

"And I'll be a monkey's oracle," muttered the raven. She winced her beak and, in a flash, her head disappeared under her left wing, where she quickly located a nibbling flea. The tiny creature was soon pulverised in her snapping jaws.

"Arr, here's our turnoff."

Bone slowed the automobile to a smooth crawl as it approached the small road sign coming into view. His eyes flashed when he read what was on it:

DELPHI MUSEUM

500 METRES

"Our celestial supermarket is but a hop, step and squawk away," the fleshy man said to his companion. "Once inside, I'm sure we'll be a lot cooler. A lot more comfortable." He let out a laugh of devious hilarity as he turned the automobile in the direction of the Museum.

Like a gaudy slug, the vehicle continued along the road. When the Museum wall appeared, Bone turned off the engine and let the car coast silently until it came to rest in front of the gates.

"Right," he said, quietly and authoritatively. He reached over the seat and tore open the lid of his clothing trunk, which lay on the back seat. He swept the mustard-coloured fez with the burgundy tassel from his head, threw it into the trunk, and withdrew another one – a sapphire-hued model with a gaudy tartan ribbon for its tassel. This he plonked onto his greasy, receding hair. He slipped off his driving gloves (casting a fast eye over all his fingernails as he did so), and threw them into the trunk as well. Then, after an elaborate display of stretching and squeezing, he got out of the car and lit a cigar.

Desdemona watched all of this and then belched.

"You uncultured flutterer," sneered Bone. "Now, quick, hop it. I need to get the alabastron."

He ambled around to the passenger side and raised the leather seat. "Come to Daddy, my little beauty," he purred. Clenching his cigar in his teeth, he lifted out a small wooden box and set it gently down upon the bonnet. With moist, pudgy fingers he carefully prised off the box's lid. Inside, cushioned in layers of high-grade straw, lay the Sacred Alabastron of Cronus.

"Arrrrrrr," breathed Captain Neptune Bone, blowing a shaft of smoke all over the ancient pottery. "Let us set about our business." He plucked up the alabastron and squeezed it into an outer pocket of his waistcoat. "Come, Desdemona. Let us start to glimpse the powers of what we have obtained."

Without a squawk, the raven fluttered from the mudguard and came to rest grottily on his round shoulder. In silence, the pair ascended the darkening stairs leading to the Museum's single bronze door.

"Right," Bone muttered, eyeing the black keyhole. "Should be a piece of meringue."

Desdemona's eyes throbbed eagerly.

He reached into the inside of his waistcoat and withdrew his third-favourite nail file. This he placed slowly into the keyhole, taking care to make as little sound as possible. When he had inserted it almost to its

full length, he rumbled like a well-fed cat. "Arrr. Primitive lock, this. Not like those ones on the Cairo Museum. This one's a cinch!"

"Hurry up, before someone comes!"

"All in good time, you impatient improbability." He held his fingers admiringly in front of him and quickly wiggled them about, until there was a loud cracking of his knuckles.

"Eeeerrrgh!" moaned Desdemona, who hated hearing this noise almost as much as she hated being rent-free accommodation for fleas.

The fingers on Bone's right hand curled slowly around the end of the nail file. With a frenzied jiggling he moved the file up and down, backwards and forwards, right and left inside the lock.

Fifteen seconds later there was a dull, echoing *click*. The sound was, to Captain Neptune Bone's ears, like a triumphant chord at the end of a monstrously long symphony.

"Right!" He pulled out the file and gently placed the palms of his fatty hands flat against the door. With no sound at all, he pushed open the door of the Delphi Museum, and slipped himself and the raven within.

Inside, all was dim. Some faint, last rays of sunlight, which had entered the Museum through the many skylights above, had been trapped within the tall walls; their remaining beams shimmered weakly, as though they were confused about how to get out again.

Bone swiftly shut the door. "Hop down, Desdemona," he ordered.

The bird did so, her talons squealing on the marble floor as she came to land. "Drat these skiddy floors," she spat, trying to stay upright as her legs started to act like items of lost property attempting to be found again.

"Stop playing the fool and come here." He reached out with one hand and grabbed her by the scruffeathers of her neck, and with the other he took out a thick red candle from his plus-fours. "Here, hold this."

"Hmm, nice colour. Goes with my peepers, don't you think?"

"Shh!" He clicked open the lid of his silver cigar-lighter, and the flame shot high into the air, sending a crazy, dancing glow up the walls and onto the skylights. He turned the flame down and set it to the wick of Desdemona's candle. Then he lifted the burning wax cylinder until it was hovering above her skull.

"What … what are you—YEEAARRRRGGGHHH!"

Bone had tipped the candle slightly, so that four large dollops of molten wax had dripped off the top and onto her head, where they had singed her feathers with a loud hiss.

"Stop whining, and help to illuminate my grandeur." He set the candle the right way up again and, with a heavy hand, plonked it straight onto the bird's skull. Here he held it firmly for several seconds until the molten wax cemented it into place.

"Let there be light." He smiled.

"Ooooh," moaned Desdemona, her eyeballs throbbing as though electrical current was pumping through them, while a handful of startled fleas jumped down onto her beak and took a stunned refuge in her cheekfeathers.

"And now, the altar."

"What? Don't you think you've altered me enough?" Desdemona took a skidding step away from him. "You tried to alter me into an ornithological torch a second ago. What have you got in that evil mind of—?"

"No, gormless, an *altar*. An object of worship."

The raven let out a sigh of relief, and fell bang onto her tarsus as her legs slipped away from underneath her.

"Be careful, that's our only candle! Now follow me. And don't dawdle!"

She shot him a filthy, slitted-eyed glare and went half-hopping, half-fluttering after him.

Through the first couple of galleries they crept, the candlelight shooting up the walls whenever Desdemona lost her clawing. All was silent; all was watchful; all of the statues and marble friezes were witness to the intruders' presence.

Presently Bone turned a corner and came into a long, high-ceilinged room. He stopped a few paces into this room and, reaching behind him, yanked the raven close. Her candlelight stretched far down to the middle of the space.

"Arrr. The altar room at last. Behold, Desdemona, the first piece of our collecting puzzle!"

In the dead centre of the room sat a large, rectangular,

waist-high block of marble, green and mottled with age. Long ago, it had been carved into the shape of an altar – a simple altar, yet majestic all the same. The top ends were formed in a scroll-like effect; between them, the flattened surface contained nothing more than a small, hollowed-out depression, circular in shape and dark in the centre.

With quiet steps, Bone approached it. "Yes, yes, yes," he whispered sibilantly. "Just as it was described by that Hattbocks dame. There, there before us, are the three narrow steps leading up to it. Oh, behold the simple lines, and those elegant volutes on the sides. Ohhhhh …' And he skipped up to it and ran his fingers in an almost disgusting manner all over the stone.

"Crark! It's just a lump of rock. What's there to get so excited about?"

"I'll show you." Bone put his tongue back into his mouth and took the Sacred Alabastron of Cronus carefully from his waistcoat. "Watch this, you doubting dum-dum." He held the alabastron high above his head, and then, slowly, slowly, ever so slowly, he lowered it towards the top of the altar, until its base was positioned directly above the hollowed-out circle. "See? It will be a perfect fit!"

Desdemona jumped up onto the scroll-work on the left-hand side and peered at the alabastron, then at the depression, then at the alabastron again. A blob of hot wax dripped onto her beak. "Arrgh! So what if it *is* a perfect fit? Why don't you just plonk it in there and be done with it?"

"Oh no, no, no," said Bone, snatching the alabastron away again and sliding it back into his pocket. "Now is not the time, nor is it the location."

"Go on, go on, just shove it in. Then we can vamoose and I can get some tins of succulent, imported Japanese seaweed and—"

"Patience is a virtue, Desdemona. So is cleanliness and obedience. You'd be well advised to remember all of those things, because, after I have staged the Divine Opening Ceremony, the order of things will be changing."

"What poppycock dost thou spout? 'The Divine Opening Ceremony'? You're addled!"

"Shut that blasphemous beak of yours, before I enwax it shut. For your information – though I can't see how you could possibly retain such world-transforming knowledge in that piddling little excuse for a skull of yours – we need to take this altar, along with several other objects of antiquity, to a certain location before we can use it, and the other ancient objects, to open the alabastron. If we were simply to attempt such a thing here, there's no predicting what manner of dreadful calamities might take place."

"It all sounds barmy, if you ask me."

"Yes, bird, you might be right. But many great schemes in this neverending procession of History have often seemed 'barmy', before they reached their fruitions. Witness Mr Thomas Alva Edison with the light-bulb. Witness Madame Marie Curie with her radium. And Mr Alexander Graham Bell with that telephonic instrument. Not to mention Countess Ingrid Von Naffschtullen and her Clockwork Miniature Earwax Spoons. We must have faith, that is all. When have I ever let you down in the past?"

Desdemona's rough, yellow tongue darted out and she licked her beak. "The Valley of the Kings – on seven occasions; Peru; under the Red Sea; Burma; Sumatra; Turkey; the jungles of Mexico; Emnob—"

"That's enough. We're wasting precious time with all this stultiloquence. Let's get this altar out of here."

It was then that something occurred to the bird. She rolled her eyeballs into the top of her head and opened her beak wide. Then she let out a long, loud cackle of derisive hilarity.

"Ah—HA-CRARK-HA-CRARK-HA-CRARK-HA-CRARK-HA-CRARK-HAHAHAHAHAHA-HAHAHAHAHAHAHAHA-CRAAARR-RRKKKK!"

"And what," growled Bone when her mirth had begun to subside, "is giving you so much pleasure?"

She raised her wings and wiped the tears from her cheekfeathers. "You, you great, hasty genius. There's one simple little thing you seem to have forgotten. One teensy, weensy detail has slipped past that thinking-factory you keep locked away under your fez. One all-important detail…"

Bone inspected his fingernails disdainfully. "Oh, yes? And what, oh putrid predictor, might that be?"

She hopped all about the top of the altar, sending

squirts of wax flying. "Take a look at my little stage," she crowed. "Notice something about it? It's big. No, it's *very* big! It's even bigger than your stomach! And it's solid, unlike your stomach. Solid marble. All the way through. Marble and marble and marble."

"It's thick, like your head. So what?"

"So, how on the planet earth do you intend to move it? It'd take an army!"

Now it was Bone's turn to laugh. He threw back his head and roared, his ginger-brown beard and moustache bristling as the air sailed through them. Then he stopped and stared at her, his eyes blazing boldly.

"Don't you worry about a thing, my little fiend. I have thought of everything, being the genius what I am. In a few short moments, you will behold not only the means of how we are to move this altar, but also the very First of the Miracles of Captain Neptune Bone. Arrrrrrrr!"

And, much louder than before, his awful laughter filled the Museum.

"In ancient times, the Greeks considered that Delphi was the very centre of all the worlds," cried Euripides Doodah, as he sat swaying and bouncing and clinging to Cairo Jim. "Do you know what my ancient forebears used to call the area all around Delphi?"

"The navel of the universe?" thought Brenda with a lumbering snort.

"The navel of the universe?" said Jim.

"Exactly!" Euripides smiled. "I see you know your Greek history well. You didn't need me to come along after all."

"Rark!" Doris, sitting at the front of Brenda's saddle, turned her head and spoke over her wing. "Don't bet on it, buddy-boy. You needed to get out more!"

It had so far been a hot, but swift, journey. Now that the sun had set, an almost full moon had taken its place, and the countryside was bathed in a strong, warm glow. The millions of olive trees all around them shimmered silently in the moonwash.

For Euripides, it had also been an uncomfortable journey, but, after the first hour or so, he had started to forget his nether portions and had begun to be fascinated by all that was around him: the outlying suburbs of Athens, which had gradually led into steep roads surrounded by mountainous slopes, and small villages scattered here and there. Until nightfall, he had seen all of this wide-eyed, despite Doris's best efforts at sending him to sleep by repeatedly turning her head and looking directly at him while she opened her beak and snapped it shut.

All at once the quiet of the evening was pierced by another of Doris's boisterous outbursts. "REEEERRRRK!"

Jim jumped in the saddle. Euripides jumped as well. Brenda jumped in the middle of her pace.

"What is it, my dear?"

The macaw pointed with her wing. "Look, down there, by that dirt track. See, in the middle of all those trees. There's something gleaming!"

Jim pulled slowly on Brenda's bridle. "Whoa, my lovely," he coaxed. The Wonder Camel slowed until she had stopped completely, and the archaeologist-poet reached down into his knapsack in her saddlebag.

"What is it, Miss Doris?" asked Euripides.

"Too far away to see clearly." She blinked rapidly. "It's big, bloated even, and shining, and it seems to be squatting … Jim, I think it's Bone himself!"

"Let's have a proper look and find out." Jim had pulled out his binoculars and now he raised them to his eyes. "Hmm." He slowly adjusted the focus. "Well, starch me rigid and call me a Corinthian column!"

"Let me see," Doris flapped. "Please, please, please!"

"Certainly, my dear."

He handed the binoculars to her and she squinted through them. "Oh, how tasteless."

"Is it Bone, Cairo Jim? What's he up to, out there in the middle of all those trees?" Euripides stopped and shuddered. "Oh, no, don't tell me – I can *quite* imagine."

"No," said Jim, "it's not Bone. Unfortunately."

"Then what?"

"It appears to be a rather large, over-inflated, cheap-looking, velvet-clad, blow-up comfy chair."

"Comfy chair?"

Jim took out his handkerchief and wiped the back of his neck. "Yes, a comfy chair. And a bulging, inelegant one at that. Only one man would possess such a piece of gross portable furniture."

"Quaaoo!" Brenda gave an impatient snort.

"Yes, you're right, my lovely." Jim took up her reins and dug his heels firmly but harmlessly into her sides. "Bone's been here. And he's scarpered off to Delphi, all right!"

"Step on it, Bren!" Doris flapped a wing against Brenda's flank as they tore into the night. "There's some mighty big fluff to be cleaned out of that old navel!"

9

THE FIRST MIRACLE

"YEERGH," shuddered Desdemona, as she and Bone crept through the dark chambers of the Museum. "This place is giving me the willies."

"Whatever are you droning on about?"

"All these statues. Look at the way they're watching us. They're making my feathers hackle, and the fleas don't like that. Ouch."

"Don't be any more moronic than you are normally, Desdemona. How can they be watching us? They're only chunks of marble and bronze."

"They … they look as if they could snake a move at any moment." Suddenly she stopped in her tracks. "CRAAAARRKK!"

Bone quickly clutched at his chest. "What is it, you excitable effluence? What's the—?"

"Look." She waved a wing at a figure at the far end of the chamber in which they had halted. "That one there, the green one with the human eyes. I saw it move!"

In the glow from Desdemona's candle, Bone peered into the gloom. His eyes narrowed, and a smile appeared on his flabby lips. "Ah, the Charioteer."

"The—the Charioteer?"

"One of the finest bronze statues ever rescued from

Greek antiquity. See? It's almost entirely intact. Only missing its arm."

"Where's that?"

"Probably in the same place as his chariot. In the ditch by the side of History's Path of Forgetfulness."

"He's a spook, if ever I saw one."

"What's the matter, Desdemona? Scared of a little bit of statuary?"

The raven lifted an eyebrow and glared at her cohort. "Me? Scared? Nevermore! I'm just delicate, that's all."

"About as delicate as a dose of bubonic plague. Come, it's not the *Charioteer* we want. We have our eyes set on greater booty to help us shift the altar."

Desdemona scowled at Bone as he disappeared around the corner. She stood for a moment, alone with the Charioteer, until her feathers started to hackle again. Then she hopped off after Bone.

They entered a room that was almost empty, except for one single statue standing in the centre, behind a knee-high barrier rope. Bone let out a gasp of delight when he beheld this statue, and he approached it speedily, his fat legs almost running.

With trembling thighs he stood before it, obstructing Desdemona's view. She half-hopped, half-fluttered to join him, being careful not to skid over on the floor or let her candle go out.

"Well, pluck me madly and call me Pinkie," she crowed when she saw the statue unobscured.

It was of a man, the biggest, the tallest, the most

gargantuan man that either Bone or Desdemona had ever seen. It stood with its feet apart, its massively muscled legs solid and column-like, its enormous chest and pectoral muscles bulging as though there were sacks of rocks piled up underneath the shiny, white marble skin. Both of its arms were stretched up towards the skylights, and its astonishingly numerous biceps seemed to be rippling like waves on the ocean. The man's face was calm, yet there was a curiosity etched across it, an almost *angry* curiosity, as though he had been trapped inside this marble layer and was demanding to know the reason why.

As Desdemona eyed the figure up and down, it seemed to her that even his neatly curled *beard* was bristling with muscles.

"Arrr," Bone whispered delightedly. "Desdemona, I'd like you to meet Herakles, the strongest man in ancient Greece. Mr Herakles will be our travelling companion from this moment forth."

The raven looked up at Bone, and her beak curled mockingly. "You've finally done it, haven't you?"

"Finally done what?"

"You've finally flipped, that's what. You've finally thrown away your last scrap of sanity. You've finally decided you're one fez short of a hat shop. Ha ha ha ha ha ha. Captain Neptune Flannelbottom Bone has lost it all, he's gone LOONY, here in some dreary little Museum with no one around to watch. Ha ha ha ha ha ha!"

Bone listened to her in silence.

"Ha ha ha h—why are you listening to me in silence?"

"Because I am amazed by you, Desdemona. You astound me."

"Oh, well, thank you very much, I ... *why*?"

"Your capacity for foolishness is limitless." She didn't know whether to take that as a compliment or an insult.

"You think," continued Bone, "that we are going to haul away old Herakles here by ourselves? That not only will we have that massive and mercilessly heavy altar to cart around, but also *him* as well?" He jerked his manicured thumbnail at the statue.

"Well, that's what it looks like."

"Let us see if the scheme of things, as it appears to your incredibly acute sense of comprehension, contains some secrets you might not know about."

He reached into his waistcoat and took out the Sacred Alabastron of Cronus. "This," he purred, holding it between his thumb and index finger, "will eventually give me more power than any other human being in all the history of all the world's civilizations, both real and mythical. Unfortunately, however, I cannot tap into that power yet ... not until I have opened this precious little vessel. Hence our need for the altar. And hence our further need for the strength of Mr Herakles here. But there *is* some power associated with this alabastron that I can utilize here and now. Helena Hattbocks wrote about it in that very helpful little book of hers." Bone licked his lips and smiled. "Stand back, my raven, and behold the *miraculous!*"

Desdemona obeyed, hopping quickly backwards.

Then, by the crazy, dancing light of the candle, Neptune Bone lifted the alabastron to his lips. His mouth moved quickly, uttering some words close to the stopper of the vessel, words that Desdemona could not recognize. The utterance was followed by Bone rotating the palm of his hand around the stopper three times, before holding the alabastron out in front of his chest.

What happened next was so astonishing that Desdemona and Bone would remember it for the rest of their days. Slowly and without a sound, the mighty figure of Herakles began to lower its arms. Down they came, as though they were moving through invisible ropes of time, ropes that had trapped them in the air for thousands of years. And, when those strong hands were resting against the colossal thighs, the head of Herakles turned even more slowly, almost as if it were pushing through a heavy but unseen fog, until the statue's unblinking marble gaze rested on the plump, fez-wearing man and his candle-wearing bundle of feathers.

"Arrrrr!" Bone was wobbling with delight. "Welcome, oh ancient Herakles. I am your master, Captain Neptune Bone. You will know and think of me as your Everlasting Omnipotence."

"Everlasting Omnipotence?" blurted Desdemona. "What poppycock—?"

"Shut up," Bone hissed from the side of his mouth.

"Don't confuse the big boy."

The statue's head moved slowly, in the direction of the short, smudgy thing on the floor. Then, without warning, Herakles stepped forward, through his barrier ropes, and took a wide swipe at the bird.

"AAAAARRRRKKK!" she screeched, flying into the air and out of his reach.

Bone stepped back, but spoke up promptly. "Steady on, big boy, don't get your toga in a twist. She" – he pointed up at the terrified raven – 'is part of my Divine Entourage. Do not be alarmed by her. She is harmless, though full of fleas."

Herakles lowered his arm, his face showing no emotion or change of expression.

"She is our … *friend*." Bone shuddered at the word.

Herakles moved his heavy head to the side, as if trying to understand.

"Our *associate*." Bone slipped the alabastron into his pocket once again, and then brought both his hands together over his heart, to illustrate the concept.

When Herakles saw this, he nodded, once and slowly.

Desdemona swooped warily down and came to rest on Bone's fez. Herakles regarded her with indifference. "You mean to say that that brute is coming with us?" she spat. "He almost crushed me to smithereens!"

"This 'brute' is going to carry our necessary accoutrements," Bone answered smugly. "Those little things we need to collect along the way in order to perform the Divine Opening Ceremony. Aren't you, Herakles, you breathtaking bundle of bulk?"

Herakles stared at them but said nothing.

"What's the matter?" croaked Desdemona. "Has the Sphinx got his tongue? Why doesn't he answer?"

"How *can* he answer? Look at those lips, they're made of solid marble. Not a sound can escape through those. Mr Herakles will be the perfect travelling companion, all right." Bone gestured to Herakles, then to the doorway. "Now, we must go, my servant. Come, follow your Everlasting Omnipotence."

"Oh, brother," muttered the raven.

With a confident, pomp-like gait, Bone left the room. Herakles walked stiffly after him, his heavy marble feet smacking loudly against the cold marble floor. Through the rooms and galleries and chambers they travelled, until they were back in the altar room.

Bone pointed at the altar. Herakles came to stand next to him, and his gaze followed the line of Bone's outstretched hand. He looked at the altar, then slowly at Bone, then slowly at the altar once again.

"Lift," Bone said. "Onto your shoulder." He motioned with his arms and hands what he wanted Herakles to do.

The marble man looked back to Bone and regarded him for several long, stunningly silent seconds. Then he advanced to the altar, like a wall on the move.

"You see?" Bone whispered. "He'll do whatever I tell him. I have full control. Arrr."

The marble around Herakles's knees glowed in the candlelight as he squatted beside the altar. His arms stretched out so that he was embracing the enormous rectangular slab. With a huge flexing of the muscles in his sculpted back, he took the strain and stood, hoisting the altar firmly onto his shoulder. There was a loud scraping of marble against marble as he balanced it.

"Oh, where have you been all my life?" Bone muttered delightedly. "Come, my man," he beckoned bossily.

He turned on his heel and, with Desdemona still perched worriedly atop his fez, he went through the corridors until he had almost reached the front door of the Museum. Before they arrived at it, however, he took a sharp turn left and led the marble man into another gallery.

"Crark! This isn't the way out. Where are we – aarrrrrgh!"

Desdemona's beak froze wide open and her flame flickered wildly as she beheld the piece of sculpture before them. It was not as big as Herakles, but it was grotesque – a thing from a nightmare, from a world that should never have existed. It sat, stonily perched on a tall pediment, fiercely but immovably surveying the strangers in the gallery.

"You're … you're not going to bring *that* to life as well, surely?" rasped the bird. "It's repulsive!"

"Coming from you, that's like the pot calling the kettle tarnished. Fear not, cowardly quills, it won't be

brought to life tonight. We're taking it, though. Mr Herakles here can put it on his other shoulder." Bone turned and, by gesturing, instructed Herakles to fetch the statue. Herakles gave a laboured nod and proceeded to do so.

"But why?" squawked Desdemona. "You put the breath of existence into *that* and it'll rip us all to shreds!"

"I doubt it. Not when I will have full control."

"Why do you want the monstrosity?"

Bone watched smugly as Herakles reached up and dragged the creature from off the pediment and settled it onto his other shoulder. "Let's just say that it will be my 'heavy artillery'. Just in case I need some. Arrrrrrrr." He reached into the backside pocket of his plus-fours and withdrew his cigar case. With the thought of his future success tingling through his fingers, he took out a cigar and bit off the end, before lighting the foul-smelling cylinder.

In his gloating, he was completely unaware of the thing that had fluttered from his pocket when he had taken out his cigar case, and which had fallen to the floor unseen by all (excepting, of course, the ancient statues lining the walls).

MISSING PIECES

BY THE TIME THAT CAIRO JIM and company arrived at the Delphi Museum, the building was moonlit in such a steady glow that it was as though a dim spotlight was shining on it. The walls around it appeared to pulsate with an incandescence that Jim had not seen since visiting remote mountain-top sites in certain South American countries.

He brought Brenda to a smooth halt, and the Wonder Camel was relieved to rest after such a long time of flat-out activity. She gave a loud, satisfied snort, her nostrils quivering open and shut as she gulped down the still, warm air around her.

"Right," Jim announced, dropping Brenda's reins and sliding down onto the path. "Everyone off."

"Oh, I am *so* glad to hear it." Euripides leaned forward, grabbed hold of the front of Brenda's saddle, and threw one leg over her side so that he too could descend. "Not that I am one to complain, but I am certain I have blisters in places I never knew existed on my person." He rubbed his rear regions as he stood beside Jim. "What I'd give for a nice, hot cup of coffee with marshmallows in it right now."

Doris flew from Brenda's forehead and came to land

on the crown of her friend's pith helmet. "Look, look!" she squawked. "The door!"

The men and Wonder Camel looked up to the door, and a chill shot into all of their hearts, in spite of the warm night.

"It's wide open," muttered Jim.

Euripides gulped. "B–B–Bone?" he stammered.

"Well I doubt that it was Shirley Temple." Jim reached into one of Brenda's saddlebags and found his torch. "Come on, there's one way to find out."

Together they approached the silent building, Brenda's hoofs *clack-clack-clack*ing on the stone pathway. When they reached the door they stopped, and Jim turned on the torch, pointing the strong beam inside.

Dozens of white, frozen faces stared back, their expressions stunned by the light.

"Preeerrraaark!" Doris screeched, and Jim reached up and patted her wing.

"Steady on, my dear, they're only sculpted. Never will they hurt you." He stepped inside, followed by Euripides and Brenda. "That felon's been here all right," he whispered, guiding the beam around the walls and watching where it fell. "See those marks on the floor?"

"Goodness," Euripides said.

Brenda bent her head low and had a close-up inspection.

"Hmm," observed Doris. She fluttered from Jim's hat and landed on the marble floor, her claws skidding a little on contact. She found her balance and then, with careful measure, lowered her head so that her beak and eyes were close to the floor, and squinted at the strange, wedge-like marks lit up by Jim's torch. "Well, I'll be a headdress for Gloria Swanson," she cooed.

"What are they?" asked Jim.

"Hard to tell. Looks like … no, couldn't be."

"Couldn't be what?" asked Euripides.

The macaw raised her head. "They couldn't be *footprints*. I mean, for goodness' sakes, this floor's marble. Who could ever make footprints in a marble floor? But, by my beak, that's what they look like, all right."

Jim ran his upper teeth over his lower lip.

"Bone's a heavy man, we know that for sure, but he can't possibly be *that* heavy!"

"He is weighted down by his own malevolent desires," Euripides frowned.

"Quaaooo!"

"What is it, my lovely?"

Brenda, who was standing close to the entrance of a chamber that led off from the room in which they were all gathered, rolled her head in a wide, circular motion.

"I think she wants us to go in there," said Euripides.

"That she does," Jim said, leading the way after her as she disappeared around the corner.

In this chamber Cairo Jim directed his torchbeam all the way down to the far wall. "There's … there's nothing here," he whispered.

"Oh, yes there is." Euripides, now that he was back inside the walls of a Museum, spoke with his old

authoritative tones, tones that had been replaced by uncertain blurtings since he had left his well-loved confines back in Athens. "Look over there." He strode off towards the fallen barrier rope.

"See?" he held up one end of the rope. "This is an Official Standard Greek Archaeological Museum Barrier Rope, as issued by the Hellenic Branch of the Antiquities Squad." He held it against his cheek, and his eyes filled with a fond remembrance. "I *know* these sorts of ropes well. They protect all that I hold great and dear from the grubby little hands of sticky fingered gawpers and sightseers. How I miss my—"

Jim raised his eyebrows.

"Oh, forgive me, Cairo Jim, Miss Doris, Miss Brenda. I just darted up the road of recollection, I am so sorry." He let the rope fall. "This rope would have been guarding something very precious from all who came to touch."

"But what?" wondered Jim, shining his light on the empty floor.

"Scraark! This!" Doris was flapping near a knee-high plinth that had a brass plaque stuck at the top.

Jim came to her and lit up the words on the plaque. "Go on, read it, my dear."

The macaw cleared the afternoon's and the night's dust from her throat and began to read clearly: "*Herakles, the strongest man in Ancient Greece. Early Classical period, 460–450 BC – possibly from Aegina.*"

Euripides gasped. "He's taken Herakles? But why?

What could he possibly want with a statue of Herakles?"

"The no-good, thieving blob of rudeness," Doris squawked.

Jim spoke quietly. "He's up to queer mischief this time, all right."

"QUAAAOOO!" Brenda's snort came loudly and urgently from a different room. Without hesitation, Jim, Doris and Euripides rushed to find her.

The Wonder Camel stood by another low plinth. "Shine your light over here, Jim," she implored telepathically, rolling her head towards the brass plaque at the top of the plinth. The archaeologist-poet obliged as they approached Brenda.

In silence, the foursome read the inscription. All of their hearts thumped heavier as they beheld the empty space above the plinth.

"The altar," said Euripides at last. "He's got it, all right." The Keeper of the Gallery of Forgotten Gods put his hand onto Jim's shoulder. "Maybe you are correct, my friend. Maybe there is something in all of this legend business. Otherwise, why would a man go to all this plunderous trouble?"

"He would have gone to this plunderous trouble at the drop of a fez, legend or no legend," Doris preerked.

Jim nodded his head slowly. "You're right, my dear. Naughtiness such as his rarely needs an excuse, or even a reason. But I reckon this legend – or, this *sequence of events that happened so long ago*, as I prefer to think of it – is shaping Bone's deeds here. Never have I known his villainy to be so daring, so *ambitious*! The altar, and Herakles … what'll he be thieving next?"

"QUAAAAOOOO!"

Jim, Doris and Euripides looked up to find that Brenda had slipped away again. Swiftly they vacated the altar room.

It didn't take long to find the Wonder Camel. There she was, in a gallery near the front door of the Museum, standing quietly in the gloom. Something white and thin was clamped in her strong jaws.

"What is it, my lovely?" Jim shone the light at her face. "What've you got there?"

"Rark! It's a bit of paper."

"A page," added Euripides, "a page from a book, if I'm not mistaken."

Doris fluttered over to Brenda and gently took the paper from her snout. She flew to Jim and, landing on his shoulder, dropped the page down into his free hand.

"Oh, Brenda, you fortuitous beast," smiled Jim. Brenda fluttered her eyelashes appreciatively, as she always did whenever her favourite human being addressed her thus.

"My friends," Jim announced, his voice rippling with the slightest smidgen of temporary triumph, "we have here the page that was torn out of Helena Hattbocks's worthy tome." He lifted the page to his nose and took a deep, long sniff. Then he screwed up his nose irritably. "Just as I thought."

"What is it?" asked Euripides.

"It reeks of two things: a strong prune-like odour, and a certain brand of cigar tobacco. 'Belch of Brouhaha', if I'm not mistaken. And we all know who smokes that brand."

"Rerk. We've smelled it in dark, vacant corners of the Old Relics Society often enough."

"Oh, by the gods, now we may be able to ascertain his next movements!" The curls on Euripides's head wobbled excitedly.

"Read on, Jim." Doris did her little flexing-up-and-down-on-his-shoulder routine.

"Let's see ... ah, yes, here we are. It begins halfway through a sentence... I think we left off where it was saying that the right kind of altar must be ... oh, yes:

"...gathered along with the other items necessary to release the Forgotten Gods during the Divine Opening Ceremony. Once the altar has been acquired, the next item to be collected is the Tripod of Tiphistiades. This small bronze tripod has been lost for the last two thousand years, and was last recorded as being used in mysterious religious ceremonies in the Rotunda of Riákia."

Euripides clasped his hands together. "Oh, yes, the Rotunda of Riákia, I have read about it often in my journals. Do you know of it, Cairo Jim?"

Jim thought for a moment. "No, I can't say I do."

"I am hardly surmised," said Euripides.

They looked at him quizzically.

"I mean, *surprised*. You see, the Rotunda's existence has largely been kept something of a secret. Only certain Museum journals carry news of it every now and then. The general public has no idea of its whereabouts. Not even many *archaeologists* know of it."

"But why not? What's so special about it?"

Euripides dropped his voice to a whisper. "It is the most complete, the most vast, the most *beautiful* ancient Greek rotunda. Its roof went long ago, but the rest is in its original state. Of course, I have not seen the Rotunda in real life, but I have carefully perused the photographs which are published from time to time. It looks magnificent. Do you know that all of its precisely straight, towering columns – eighty-seven of them, to be exact – are still arranged in the same perfect circle in which they were erected more than two thousand years ago? It is one of the constant sources of amazement to my Museum colleagues and myself that the Rotunda is still standing. So many similar ancient rotundas have long been destroyed, by invading armies, or landslides, or even earthquakes. But not the Rotunda of Riákia."

"And is that why it's such a secret? So that it won't be swarming with sightseers or pilferers the like of Neptune Bone?"

"Yes, I would say that is the reason. To ensure its continued preservation. I *know* it is a shame; I *know* that many people would like to behold such a marvel of ancient architecture, but ... well, here in Greece, we have lost so much already, what with plunderers and natural disasters. We only want to hold on to what little we have left, for as long as we possibly can."

"I understand," nodded Cairo Jim.

"Rark!" Doris squawked sadly.

"Ah, yes, Miss Doris, I can tell you many tales of injustice concerning our ancient monuments."

"Where exactly is the Rotunda of Riákia located?" Jim asked.

"To the north," replied Euripides, his dark eyes lighting up. "Quite a way from here, a little north-west of Katerini. The Rotunda is hidden between some low hills, in a place where nobody lives and where the local folk seldom visit. Oh, to think that I will be lucky enough to see it! Never in my wildest dreams—"

"Right," said Jim, who, while Euripides had been talking, had taken from the satchel in Brenda's saddlebag the map of Greece that Gerald Perry Esquire had provided for them. This the archaeologist-poet unfolded and studied closely. "Yes, you're right, it *is* quite a way. And Bone's probably got a good head-start on us." He looked up at Brenda. "My lovely, with your help, we could be there by mid-morning tomorrow. Are you up to riding through the night?"

Brenda the Wonder Camel looked at her friend's pleading eyebrows, and her other friend's pleading crestfeathers, and her newest friend's pleading curly bits on the top of his head. Without even having to think about it, she moved *her* head in a big circle, and snorted loudly.

"QUAAAOOO!"

Jim smiled; Doris clapped her wings, and Euripides did a little jig, which he quickly brought under control before it got out of hand.

In a flash of time, Jim and Euripides were on Brenda's saddle, and Doris was perched on top of Jim's pith helmet. With a clatter of hoofs on marble, the tireless Wonder Camel was out through the Delphi Museum's open door and away into the dark, northwards-beckoning night.

The large black automobile had arrived silently just seconds before Brenda had carried her company off. The driver was stepping out of the vehicle when he was alerted by the sound of her hoofbeats.

At first, judging from the loudness, he thought the beast was coming towards him. But, as he recognized the silhouetted shadows spreading against the light-coloured stone wall, he realized they were heading in the opposite direction.

As the silhouettes disappeared up the night-swaddled north road, Chief Inspector Reg Apollo (of the Hellenic Branch of the Antiquities Squad) reached into the glove compartment of his car and fished out his small, spiral-bound Antiquities Squad Regulation Issue Notepad. He flicked open the front cover and, on the first clean page he came to, began to write:

Camel – positively identified & known as "Brenda the

Wonder Camel". Eyelashes: notable. Prolific snorter. No known aliases.

Macaw – positively identified & known as "Doris". Feathers: blue & gold, lots of them. Habitual squawker, often screeches. No known aliases.

Man – identity unknown to this Officer.

Man – positively identified & known as "Cairo Jim". Occupation: archaeologist (professional), poet (non-professional). Member, Old Relics Society, Cairo, Egypt. Frequent pith helmet & special desert sun-spectacles wearer. Sometimes also known as "Jim of Cairo".

When Chief Inspector Reg Apollo had finished his jottings, the subjects of his attentions had long vanished into the darkness. With a sigh, Apollo put the Antiquities Squad Regulation-Issue Notepad into the inside pocket of his linen blazer. Then he strode briskly up the Museum path to inspect the scene of nocturnal plunder.

11

THE INNER CREVICES
OF NEPTUNE BONE

DESDEMONA THE RAVEN was snoring loudly, even though the sun had already risen high in the sky. She lay on the back seat of the blue Bugatti, one wing sprawled across her eyes, her rough and yellow tongue hanging out of her beak and dribbling most unfortunately onto the leather upholstery. She looked like a horribly feathered handbag that somebody of good taste had sensibly discarded.

Nearby, the hulking white figure of Herakles sat stock-still on a boulder, staring blankly ahead. Next to the boulder sat the altar and next to that, Captain Neptune Bone's "heavy artillery".

Occasionally a butterfly would come to land on Herakles' shoulder, where it would flicker innocently until the statue's swiping arm would create a hurricane-like turbulence of air, and the confused little creature would fly off into the clear, country sky.

Bone himself was kneeling on the grass next to his automobile, his rear looking like two generous hills covered with plaid. He had driven all through the night, with Herakles, heavy burdened and silent, lumbering obediently behind the car.

When they had arrived at this place, the overblown archaeologist had settled down for what he believed were a few well-deserved hours of shuteye, but had soon woken in a cold sweat when a nasty nightmare had come upon him. (It had involved his being awarded First Prize in the Old Relics Society's Annual Mae West Lookalike Competition, and his winning outfit had caused a dreadful rash all over his substantial loins. That bit hadn't caused his alarm – it was the choice of colour of the frock he was wearing during the prize-giving ceremony.)

Unable to get back to sleep, he had lit a cigar and, deciding to have a little read, he had reached into his pocket for the Helena Hattbocks page. Hence the reason for his kneeling on the grass.

All around him were scattered the contents of his pockets: his beloved manicure kit, the case tastefully engraved with an intimate inscription from his beloved mother; one leather-bound cigar case, three-quarters full of "Belch of Brouhaha" cigars; half a dozen sticks of extra-effective liquorice; a small, sticky Cellophane bag of squashed prunes; a tiny silver-framed portrait of his mother and himself when he was younger and less hirsute around his jowls (and when she was too); his gold fob-watch and chain; a folded catalogue from Omar Darling's Clementine Hat Shoppe with full-colour advertisements of the latest available styles in fezzes; a spare manicure kit; an inflatable donkey; a pocket-size brochure of exotic tattoos; a telescope (*that* had taken some getting out of his hip pocket); some ivory toothpicks; his silver cigar-lighter; several hair-combs, some greasy and others barely used; a slightly torn photograph of Jocelyn Osgood – Chief Stewardess of Valkyrian Airways and "good friend" of Cairo Jim; a compact sewing kit; a pamphlet entitled *Stun that Raven! Party Tricks for the Discerning*; a gold tiepin with a large diamond set in the centre; an extra spare manicure kit; some crumpled outstanding dues notices from the Old Relics Society; seven small bottles of Special Men's Fragrance he had bought in a dimly lit shop near Gurna Village because he believed he was a very Special Man; a metronome; a silver soup ladle; an extra extra spare manicure kit; an antique mellophone; four postage stamps; a handful of Greek coins; a collapsible full-length dressing mirror; a bicycle pump; a slender green tube full of mysterious-looking capsules; an extra extra extra spare manicure kit; and, finally, a length of string – "a good bit of string" – which, in keeping with the Society's code, he always carried about with him because he never knew when it might come in handy.

Captain Neptune Flannelbottom Bone did not hold with the whole idea of "the willing suspension of disbelief". He did, however, believe that a man of means deserved as many pockets as he could afford.

Despite this, nowhere could he find the piece of paper he was so desperately and frantically seeking. And now, as he pulled out the final object from the last internal crevice of his clothing – an extra extra extra extra spare manicure kit, which he'd pinched from a market in

Villahermosa – his loss was driving him out of his fez.

"Arrrrrrr!" he cried loudly to the stillness of the morning. "Where in tarnation has it got to?"

Herakles turned his head slowly at the sound of Bone's anguish. Although he could not hear as humans could, he could feel vibrations of sound against his body.

"Never you mind yourself, you marble macho man," sneered Bone. "You wouldn't have a single clue as to anything in that dense and sculpted bonce of yours."

Herakles stared at the desperate figure for a few moments, then turned sadly and silently away.

"It should be HERE!" exclaimed Bone, running his pudgy hands over all the objects before him, turning over the smaller, lighter bits and pieces and peering earnestly underneath them. "But no, ALAS, no no no no no! Oh, when I become one of the Immortals myself I shall not let a thing such as this happen to me. No fear, when I am the Divine Everlasting Omnipotence, Father of All That Will Be, why, I shall OUTLAW THE WHOLE CONCEPT OF CARELESSNESS." He grunted and rose to his feet and shook his ball of a fist at the heavens. "AAAAAAARRRRRRRRR, MARK MY VERY WORDS!"

"Craaarrrrrrk!" A black, tatty wing appeared over the door of the Bugatti, followed by a heavily blinking pair of slitted eyes. "What in the name of Zasu Pitts is that dreadful noise?"

Bone bent over and snatched up his cigar lighter and a cigar. He quickly bit off the end of the cigar, spat it at the bird (it was a good shot and bounced off her skull), shoved the cigar in his mouth, and lit it fiercely. After he had exhaled a long shaft of smoke, he straightened his fez and sauntered over to her. "I'm so sorry. Did I upset your sleepies? Oh, how *rude* of myself. How ever will you *pardon* me?"

"Well," yawned the raven, "if you were to get down on those knees of yours – you remember them, my Captain, even though you haven't been able to see them for years, they're those two little round bits in the middle of your—BLEEEEAAAARRRRKKK!"

Bone had grabbed her by her scrawny throat and was now lifting her out of the automobile, high above his head. "You cannot afford to be so insolent, you sickening sack of scumminess. You dare to talk of Neptune Bone on his *knees*? What irony you spout in your ignorance. You have no idea, do you, that one day the knees that shall bow will not include those of yours truly." He drew back his arm with malevolent intent. "Take a flying lesson, Desdemona, and learn some wisdom while you're up there."

And, with all his might, he hurled her far out into the sky.

For nearly a full, catapulting minute, the bird tumbled over and over through the air, unable to get her flying balance. Then a gust of wind blew into her feathers and turned her steadily up for a second; she flapped her wings, even though her head was still spinning, and soared unsteadily upwards.

She flew about for a while, regaining her equilibrium,

before descending hesitantly to land at a safe distance from Bone, who had gone to sit on the rear mudguard.

"A bit upset, are we?" she croaked warily at him.

"What gives you that impression?"

She pecked at a wingful of voracious fleas who were obviously annoyed at their sudden jaunt into space. "I don't usually enjoy such a *thrusting* start to my days, that's all."

"Yes," rumbled Bone, flicking his ash disdainfully. "I *am* most perturbed. You haven't happened to lay those throbbing eyes of yours on that scrap of paper I had on my person, have you?"

"Nope. Not since the last time you shoved it in your pocket."

"Accursed be the screen of Delight," he growled.

"I slept like a cuckoo bird," she whined, "that back seat is the most uncomfortable mattress I've ever … what time is it?"

He leaned over and plucked up his fob-watch from the grass. "Eleven-seventeen," he answered. "You slept badly?" he smiled.

"Yergh. I may as well have been sleeping on old big boy's shoulders over there." She gestured at Herakles, who was swatting at gnats all around him. "Talk about rock hard!"

"I think I may have a little something to – shall we say – 'pep you up'."

"Eh?" Desdemona squinted at him suspiciously.

"Oh, yes," he said, striding around his possessions.

From the vast array he picked up the slender green tube. With a flick of his thumb, the cap at the top of the tube shot into the air, and Bone tipped the container into the palm of his hand. When he held his hand out to Desdemona, it was littered with a dozen small, black, capsules. "Have a munch on these for a while," he purred. "I'm sure they'll give you a kick!"

"Don't mind if I do, thank you very much." She hop-fluttered over to him and gobbled the lot into her beak.

"But whatever you do, don't bite them. Suck them only, Desdemona. No sudden moves, or excitable squawkings."

"Why? What are they?"

"Gelignite capsules," answered Bone.

"G ... G ... Gelignite c–c–c–capsules?" Her panic-stricken eyes almost bulged out of her head.

"Arrr. There's enough power in them to make Kingdom Come a close reality. Under no circumstances should you swallow them. Otherwise your *end* will be your end*ing*."

"Bu," she stammered, trying to speak in such a way that her beak wouldn't chomp shut during her words, an action that made her sound like a very old raven with ill-fitting dentures, "bu hy?"

"Because, along with big boy over there, you are going to be instrumental in destroying *that* for me." He pointed down into the quiet meadow before them.

"Wha ... wha is i?" The capsules were becoming sticky in her gullet, and she had to keep moving them

THE INNER CREVICES OF NEPTUNE BONE

around with her tongue so they wouldn't set.

"The Rotunda of Riákia. The place where we must find the Tripod of Tiphistiades."

"He Ro-un-a o Ri-á-ia? He R-i-o o I-hi-sia-es?"

"You sound like a Sumo wrestler whose loincloth has been pulled up far too tight when you talk like that. Yes, Desdemona. It is lucky that I am a natural Genius and that I can remember what was written on that piece of paper. Down there is where we must look for the next part of our Celestial collection spree."

The raven kept moving her tongue timidly around the inside of her beak as she viewed the colossal ancient site before her. Set amongst the long grasses and the camomile, with the poppies and pink and white daisies sprouting everywhere between the ancient stones, stood the perfectly round Rotunda. Each of its eighty-seven columns was shining in the sunlight, and all of the inscriptions on the heavy architrave that the columns supported, and which ran around the entire radius of the building, were lit up in the splendid light.

Even Desdemona – whose taste for classical architecture rarely extended beyond gargoyles or water spouts she could knock off old buildings and sell for hers and Bone's profit – was clearly impressed. "I's an-a-sic," she mumbled under her breath.

"Arr, you think so, do you?" smiled Bone, blowing smoke at her. "Well, it won't be fantastic for too much longer. Go and fetch Mr Herakles and bring him over here for his instructions. And dally not, Desdemona, for you and he have work to do, and time is ticking uncharitably onwards."

"Wha-e-er you say, y Cap-ain."

⊡ ⊡ ⊡ ⊡ ⊡ **12** ⊡ ⊡ ⊡ ⊡ ⊡

THE DOMINO EFFECT

ON THE OTHER SIDE of the Rotunda, another small group of travellers had just arrived.

Snorting wildly and with her mane tousled from the nightlong journey, Brenda the Wonder Camel came to a much-deserved stop by the western side of the curved building. She stood still, breathing heavily and feeling the sweat rolling down her limbs, while Jim, Doris and Euripides all remained on her back, speechless and squawkless as they beheld the magnificence of the structure before them all.

After nearly three minutes of awe-struck silence, Jim dismounted.

Doris fluttered over to the round steps which led to within the Rotunda. "Have you ever seen anything like it?" she prerked, craning her neck backwards as she looked far up at the towering columns. "'The cloud-capp'd towers, the gorgeous palaces, the solemn temples,'" she prerked, quoting from Act Four of *The Tempest*. "Why, they have nothing on *this* joint!"

With a little discomfort, Euripides slid down from Brenda's saddle. "It is indeed a tholos of unsurpassed remarkableness," he whispered.

"That it is," gasped Jim. As he stood looking up at its

⦂⏚⏚⦂ **127** ⦂⏚⏚⦂

sheer perfection, he felt humbled to be able to stand by something from ancient times that had not been pulverized or plundered or pillaged. Every pore of the archaeologist-poet's skin erupted with prickling; every goosebump that emerged was filled with amazement. Behind his special desert sun-spectacles, his eyes filled with tears. "I'll just get Brenda some water," he muttered, going to her saddlebags and taking out the largest water container and Brenda's drinking bowl.

Doris turned her head to Euripides. "What's a tholos?" she asked.

"A circular building, such as this," he answered quietly, his eyes darting across the stonework that never in his wildest dreams had he imagined he would see in this world. "It is just another name for a rotunda, really."

"Coo," cooed the macaw.

Jim had poured a large bowl of water for Brenda and now he came back to join them. "It's so overwhelming, I feel like I could reach up and lick the moon. Hmm, that's a good idea for a poem, don't you think?"

"Not right now, Jim," said Doris kindly.

"Look." Euripides was pointing up at the architrave. "There's something inscribed there."

"Let's take a look, then." Doris shot off to the top of the closest column, where she hovered and squinted at the writing carved into the stone. "Hmm ... it's all Greek to me. Ancient Greek. And it goes on, right around the perimeter."

"Can you read it, Euripides?" asked Jim.

"I'll do my best," Euripides squinted.

"It might tell us something about where this tripod is," squawked Doris. "Wait a moment and I'll fly around the whole thing and have a squizz."

She took off to the right and flew steadily around the architrave, her gold and blue feathers almost sparkling in the sun as she disappeared around the curved stone. After about a minute, she came back to where she had started, and fluttered down to Jim's shoulder. "It looks like it says the same thing, over and over, all the way around. All the letters seem to be repeated, with a few dots between each group of the words."

"Ah, yes," nodded Euripides. "Now I have it. I was thrown for a bit by those 'e's, you know."

"What does it tell us?" Jim asked.

"'Only One Kind of Man Will Bring You Good Fortune When You Seek The Forgotten.'"

"Oh, well that's nice to know," Doris piped up. "But what does it mean, for heaven's sakes?"

"Search me," said Euripides.

Jim frowned. "'Only One Kind of Man Will Bring You Good Fortune When You Seek The Forgotten,'" he repeated slowly, letting the words float around his brain separately as he tried to pick up a clue from any of them. "'Only One Kind of Man...' Hmm, I'm as stumped as an obelisk."

"Rarrrk, look, there in the centre. It's some kind of—"

Euripides finished her squawk for her: "Offering stand or something. Yes, I do believe it is, carved from marble."

Brenda, having had a hearty drink and feeling slightly more rested, lumbered through the wildflowers to join them.

"Lead the way, my lovely," Jim said, as she clambered up the steps and passed between two of the columns to approach the centre of the Rotunda.

There, the foursome gathered around the solid, rectangular block of cream-coloured marble, the top edges of which were carved in a scroll-like border. In the centre of the top of the marble a neat set of words had been inscribed.

Doris blinked. "It's exactly the same as what's all around the architrave."

"'Only One Kind of Man Will Bring You Good Fortune When You Seek The Forgotten,'" recited Jim and Euripides in unison, while Brenda (whose early childhood digestion of all those volumes of the *Encyclopaedia Britannica* had stood her in good stead, especially the volume containing the information about Ancient Greek writing) *thought* it at the same time.

"They certainly wanted to get their message across, didn't they?" Doris said.

At that moment, Brenda's extra-sensitive ears pricked up. "QUAAAOOO!" she snorted urgently.

"Steady on, my lovely." Jim reached up and stroked her snout. "What is it?"

"I think she's heard something," whispered Euripides.

"Rark, what is it, Bren?"

But the distressed Wonder Camel could only look wildly around in alarm.

Bone's beard and moustache bristled with pleasure as he watched the scene below through his telescope. "Arrr, he's right on course."

"Has he go there ye?" croaked Desdemona, her tongue working double-time to keep the gelignite capsules from having any sudden contact with the interior of her mouth.

"Almost, you miserable, mangy muncher. Almost."

Striding heavily through the meadow of wildflowers, Herakles was approaching the Rotunda of Riákia. With every step he took, his heavy marble feet left deep divots in the dry ground, and swarms of butterflies shot out, terrified, from the long grasses through which he was ploughing his path.

"Yes," continued Bone, "in just a few moments we shall see if the Tripod of Tiphistiades is secreted anywhere in all that mess of columns. And if it's not, then you, my dear Desdemona, shall finish the investigation, thanks to those luscious and lethal little lozenges you have in your gruesome gob. And then I … hello, what in the name of Mother is *that*?"

His magnified gaze had spied and settled on something within the Rotunda.

"Wha's wha?"

Bone's beard and moustache stopped bristling with pleasure and were now standing on end with the

CAIRO JIM AND THE ALABASTRON

electricity of ecstasy. "Oh, what have I done to deserve such good fortune? Oh, thank you, Mother, thank you!"

"Eh? Goo for-une? Wha o you mea?"

He took his eye from the telescope and beamed. "I mean that not only will I get my way with the Rotunda of Riákia, but I shall also have the immense and long overdue pleasure of getting rid of that do-goodie-goodie Cairo Jim and his meddlesome camel and that loud and uppity macaw of his."

"Wha? Are *they* ow there?"

"They most certainly are," the large man purred. "And who's that with them? Euripides Doodah?"

"Eur-i-i-es, eh?"

"My, oh my, what a wonderful day," sang Bone. He looked down at the raven, whose beak was going in all directions as she earnestly manoeuvred her mandibles. "It looks like I may be able – if you'll forgive me being stunningly and excessively witty – to kill two birds with the one stone."

"Wai a mi-ue. You mea, the sone is Herales? An the birs?" She almost stopped her tongue moving about, as the thought struck her like a slap in the beak, and the colour drained from her feathers. "You don mea ...?"

Captain Neptune Bone threw back his head and laughed loudly into the sky.

"QUAAAAAOOOO!" snorted Brenda again, only this time much, much louder.

Cairo Jim had to take hold of her reins to stop her

from bolting. "What, Brenda? Steady on, my love—"

"Jim!" Doris jumped from his shoulder and on to the floor. "The ground!"

The curls on Euripides's head quivered, then stopped.

"What, Doris?" Jim looked puzzled.

"The ground, it moved."

Jim concentrated his attention on the marble floor beneath his boots. "Are you sure? It's perfectly still now."

"Rark, by my feathers, it moved! Like a little earth tremor!"

"QUAAAOOOOO!"

Euripides's curls quivered again. Then they stopped. "Oh, yes," he whispered. "It's happened once more, just now."

"Maybe you've both got the hiccups. Sometimes they can be very—"

"QUUUUUUUAAAAAAAAOOOOOOOO!"

"Reeraark! There it goes again."

Euripides's curls moved like they were in a short, sharp breeze.

This time, Jim felt it as well. "Well, swoggle me surreptitiously."

Then came the sound. A low rumbling, quick and sharp, like a thunder clap from several hills away. And after the rumble, the ground shuddered a further time.

"What is it?" gasped Euripides underneath his trembling curls. "An earthquake?"

Once more, the rumbling clap, louder this time, as though it was coming closer. Once more, the accompanying shudder of marble floor.

And here, Jim's blood ran cold, far colder than it should have in such a hot climate. "Oh, good gracious me," he muttered, his words hardly audible. "Doris, Brenda, Euripides, look out there!"

They all looked through the gaps between the columns. Down across the pale brown grass the gleaming marble figure of Herakles was crashing like a stupefied steamroller. Closer he came, the flowers and small bushes being crushed under his massive feet, the ground shaking unsteadily whenever he moved.

"But it's the statue Herakles," cried Euripides. "How can it be animated like this?"

"It's Bone's doing," Jim said gravely. "Watch out, it's headed this way. Come on, gang, let's take cover between the columns over there!" He yanked Brenda's bridle and they all scurried to the eastern side of the Rotunda.

"Do you think he saw us?" screeched Doris, over the crashing of the footsteps.

"I don't even know if it *can* see," answered Jim.

"What's he doing now?" Euripides asked, peering round the columns.

Jim looked around the other side. "I've lost him," he frowned uncertainly.

"He must've stopped," whispered Doris. "The ground's not moving any more."

"Quaaaooo!"

"Listen!" Jim gasped. "What's that sound?"

From the other side of the Rotunda, a low, dreadful scraping arose. The noise was short at first, but then it started getting longer as it became drawn out. At the same time, it swelled louder, until it had a dreadful, sharp hollowness to it, more dreadful than a thousand sets of teeth gnashing against each other.

"Ooh!" Euripides slapped his hands over his ears. "It's so grating! What on earth is he—?"

"Oh, no!" Jim had inched around the column until he could partially see Herakles. "He's ... he's pushing!"

"Rark! Pushing?"

"Against that column over there. If he's not careful, the whole Rotunda—"

CRAAAAACCCCCCKKKK!

The Rotunda of Riákia began to shake so violently that Jim thought for an instant that the sky had collapsed onto it. Slowly, like a mighty, ancient tree being felled, the column against which Herakles had been pushing began to teeter. To the right it swayed, then back to the left, then to the right again. And then it fell.

The noise it made as it smashed against its neighbouring column shot out across the still meadows and hills like cannon volley. Jim, Doris, Brenda and Euripides felt as though their eardrums were about to explode.

For an instant, all was quiet. Nothing seemed to move. Only the air was filled with a small wafting of

 135

crumbling stone and dust. The fallen column rested against its neighbour like a very tall, very exhausted human resting against the shoulder of a friend.

Then the chain of events took horribly over.

With a gigantic groan of shattering marble, the fallen column broke into a thousand giant pieces, and slid to the ground, causing the neighbouring column to tilt slowly to the right.

CRAAAAACCCCCCKKKK!

"Oh, no, no, no," cried Cairo Jim, his heart flooding with utter devastation. "Not this, not to this place of all places!"

The second fallen column rested against the column next to it for a split second before the pattern was repeated. As though in slow motion, this column went tilting and crashing against the next, and that against the next, and that against the next one, all of them shattering as they went.

CRAAAAACCCCCCKKKK!
CRAAAAACCCCCCKKKK!
CRAAAAACCCCCCKKKK!

In less than fifteen seconds, more than thirty of the columns were reduced to rubble.

Doris flapped her wings wildly, her squawk ricocheting into the air. "Jim! The architrave! It's disintegrating, REEERRRAAAAARRRKKKK!"

The archaeologist-poet looked quickly up, snatching off his desert sun-spectacles as a large piece of masonry from the architrave narrowly missed his forehead.

"QUUUAAAOOOOO!"

Overhead, the long, round band of the sculpted marble architrave was breaking up like thick icing around a wedding cake and plummeting onto the fallen, shattered columns.

"Look out!" screamed Euripides, his wavering hand pointing around the circle.

CRAAAAACCCCCCKKKK!
CRAAAAACCCCCCKKKK!
CRAAAAACCCCCCKKKK!

"The columns!" Jim grabbed Brenda's bridle more tightly. "They're still falling. Come on, everyone, into the centre, before we're pulverized!"

With all the haste they could muster, they raced and galloped and flew to the rectangular block of creamy, scrolled marble in the centre of the floor, far from the circular onslaught of rubble.

CRAAAAACCCCCCKKKK!
CRAAAAACCCCCCKKKK!
CRAAAAACCCCCCKKKK!
CRAAAAACCCCCCKKKK!
CRAAAAACCCCCCKKKK!
CRAAAAACCCCCCKKKK!
CRAAAAACCCCCCKKKK!
CRAAAAACCCCCCKKKK!
CRAAAAACCCCCCKKKK!

All around, column onto column continued to tilt and crack, shatter and collapse. The ancient Titans themselves may as well have been flattening a row of

Almighty Dominoes. It sounded like all the thunderbolts in the world were colliding together at once.

Throughout, something was collapsing in a like manner in Cairo Jim's heart.

The smooth marble floor was breaking up too: cracks like long, treacherous fingers zigzagged across it whenever a new column fell.

Finally, many minutes later, the noise stopped, as abruptly as it had started. Herakles was lumbering away up the hill towards his liberator, but Jim, Doris, Brenda and Euripides could not see him: the air was thick with dust and falling grit.

Brenda snorted fiercely, blowing the grains of ancient fragments from her nostrils.

Cairo Jim was dazed beyond belief. He slumped, exhausted, against the marble block – the only bit of the Rotunda of Riákia still intact – and stared through defeated eyelids at the mess that up until a few minutes ago had been one of the Unfamous Marvels of the Ancient World.

Presently, Doris coughed and spoke. "What's that?"

Euripides wiped a hand through his curls. "What is what, Miss Doris?"

"Listen." She cocked her beak to the side and concentrated.

Silently, Jim concentrated too.

"I don't hear anything," said Euripides.

"Not surprising," Doris whispered nervously. "Only a bird could hear it."

"Quaaaooo?" snorted Brenda.

"Only a bird could hear it," Doris went on, "because only a bird could make it."

"Oh," gasped Euripides, "now I hear it!" Steadily it became louder: a low droning, like a battalion of mosquitoes intent on attack. But it wasn't a battalion of mosquitoes – as Jim, Doris, Brenda and Euripides looked into the sky above them, the sun blackened for an instant. And then came Desdemona.

"She's dive-bombing," cried Jim. "Hit the marble, everyone!"

They flung themselves down and covered their heads with hands, wings and hoofs. The raven hurtled onwards, fleas flying in all directions, her red eyeballs throbbing fiercely with pleasure as she looked forward to getting rid of her unwelcome mouthful.

Just when her belly was about to skim the floor she swerved back upwards and arced once more into the air far above.

PATTOOOOOOOOEEEY!

A dozen small, black, gooey pellets shot from her mouth, missile-like towards their target.

The rectangular block of scrolled marble exploded into a million shards of creamy whiteness.

KABOOOOOOOOOOOOOOOM!

"Keep your heads down!" yelled Cairo Jim, as the pieces showered down upon them all.

"RAAAAARRRK!" screeched Doris, burying her beak deeper into her wings.

Once again, the sky blackened, and once again the raven plummeted. But this time she didn't spit a destructive gobload onto them. Instead, she swooped right into the midst of the mess, in between Jim and Doris, and with unstoppable talons she snatched up an object that had been exposed in the blast.

As Desdemona disappeared up into the settling dust, Jim saw a glint of bronze in her talons, and he knew what she was carrying: the small tripod.

The air was heavy with hopelessness and devastation.

🔲 🔲 🔲 🔲 🔲 **13** 🔲 🔲 🔲 🔲 🔲

MOCKERY OF RUBBLE

SOMEWHERE IN THE HILLS above them, an automobile roared off into the distance. As Jim started to pick himself off the cracked floor of the ruin – for now it could truly be called that – he thought he heard and felt the ground vibrating slightly. He shook his head, sending a cloud of grit flying from his hair, and retrieved his pith helmet from a pile of debris. His beloved hat was pockmarked with dents.

For many long minutes nobody spoke or squawked or snorted. Brenda rose in her steeply angled way and began to lumber through the carnage, looking dazed and confused. Doris slowly hopped about, sometimes poking her beak into the piles of broken marble, sometimes flexing and shaking her wings to rid the feathers of their powdery coatings. Euripides sat where he had dived, coughing and scratching at his curls and wishing he had a cup of steaming black coffee with marshmallows in it to revive him. He looked glumly at the torn sleeve of his blue coat.

Cairo Jim put on his special desert sun-spectacles and began to wander around the site. During the destruction, the right lens of his sun-spectacles must have been struck by flying rock, for there was a large shatter-line running diagonally across it. Looking through this crack in the glass, Jim's spirits took a turn for the worse.

How, he wondered, could such a thing be allowed to happen? Where was the reason? Where was the *justice* in things, if such a beautiful and important monument such as this Rotunda could just be smashed to smithereens, all because of the evil whims of one single man? What of the Herakles statue – had they all actually seen it moving? *Was Bone going to become one of the gods himself?*

Answers, he needed answers. But here, in this forsaken mess, it seemed that there were no answers, only unsolved questions. Jim sniffed the air. It seemed to be full of mockery.

He continued to wander through the mess, his insides empty and flat, when he stumbled on something in his path. He stopped and squatted to look at it. There in front of him lay a slab of the original architrave, a piece about three metres in length. Amazingly, that much of it had survived without being broken into hundreds of smaller pieces, like much of the rest of the architrave had been.

When he read what was written on the portion of architrave, his heart became as heavy as the rock he was viewing. Then he began to laugh.

At first he giggled, quietly and steadily, but within seconds the giggling had grown to a loud, full-throated roaring. He laughed until his eyes were watering behind his sun-spectacles, and his ribcage was aching as he tried to gulp down more air so that he could keep on laughing. Finally, unable to stop, he collapsed onto the architrave fragment, holding his sides and rocking back and forth. "Ha ha ha ha ha ha ha ha ha ha!"

Doris flew over to see what all the fuss was about. She found Jim cradling himself in his hilarity on the slab of architrave.

"Jim!" she squawked, kindly and worriedly (for she had never seen her best mate like this before). "What is it?"

Cairo Jim stopped laughing for a second and looked at her through watery eyes. Then he threw his head back and the laughter came again, hoarsely and relentlessly.

"JIM!" She hopped onto his knee and looked closely at his face. "What's so funny?"

"*Ha ha ha ha ha ha ha ha ha!*" was all he could bellow.

Doris realized he was hysterical. With her gentle wingfeathers she began to slap him lightly on the cheeks. "This is hurting me more than it is you, buddy-boy," she squawked. "Jim! Snap out of it! *Rerark!*"

Her concerned screech brought the archaeologist-poet swiftly back to reality.

"Doris," he gasped. "I've just now realized something."

The macaw looked at him, waiting for him to continue.

"Something quite ghastly," he said, smiling. "Doris, my dear, we're all done for."

She blinked sternly at him. "What? Jim, this isn't like you."

"No, it's not. But, Doris, never before have I realized that all of the Fates were working against us. It looks like, for the first time, Neptune Bone has Fortune firmly on his side." Jim paused and wiped his forehead with the back of his hand. "My dear, dear Doris, *Bone is going to win this battle.*"

"Eh? That's as silly as a wet toucan. How can you be so sure?"

"He's got his altar. And now he's got his Tripod of Tiphistiades. And look," said Jim. He moved his knees to the side, so that Doris could see the inscription on the architrave beneath him. "Read it and squawk, my dear."

Doris blinked and scanned the rock before reading aloud. "'Only One Kind of Man Will Bring You Good Fortune When You Seek The Forgot.'" (That was where the architrave had broken.) "So?" she said, confused. "We've certainly seen *this* before. So what?"

"Don't you understand? One kind of man. Bone *has* him. Bone's got *Herakles*!"

The feathers on Doris's crest arched forward and then stood on end.

"We may as well give up now," muttered Jim. "With Herakles on his side, there'll be no tomorrow!"

The macaw blinked rapidly, and peered curiously at him. "Maybe," she ventured, "the *Man* doesn't mean Herakles at all."

"Oh, yes it does, all right." Jim's laughter had disappeared completely. "It's as obvious as the pith helmet on my head."

"But we can't be sure, we don't know for cert—"

"We may as well head back to Athens and prepare for the absolute worst. Bone will very soon become a..." But he couldn't bring himself to say it out loud.

At that moment Brenda snorted excitedly. Jim and Doris did not hear her, but Euripides did; he stood and stumbled across to the Wonder Camel, who was holding something small between her powerful teeth.

"What have you got there, Miss Brenda?" he asked quietly, holding out his hand.

"Quaaaooo!" She rotated her head and fluttered her eyelashes. The small gold object dropped down into Euripides's palm.

"Oh, I am relieved someone's found *something* out of all this mess." He carefully held the signet ring up to his eye, twisting it so that the sunlight could light up the tiny figures carved into the seal. "It is very beautiful, don't you think?"

"Quaoo." Brenda's mane trilled with some new form of optimism that not even she could explain.

"Now listen to me," Doris was saying sternly to Jim. "This is no time to start giving up the ghost! Remember who you are, remember what you've accomplished. All of your archaeological discoveries, all of your successes!"

"I still haven't had any poems published," he muttered gloomily.

"But, Jim, you've made people think! You've challenged them, you've made them see that the past is a valuable thing, that History is something that we can learn from, a thing we should cherish!" She began to hop about as her words propelled her on. "Rark! Now, more than ever, that's an ideal that's going to have to be believed in, and *you're* the one who should practise what you spout. You can't just throw in the trowel, not even after all of this ... this *devastation*, and certainly not over a walking lump of stone, and that overblown greedy-guts with the worst taste in clothing this century! Think of what's at stake, you dear, dear man: not only the future of the civilized world, but also—"

Jim's eyes had started to regain their old sparkle as he had listened to his feathered friend's rousing advice. "But also my beliefs, my ideals," he said gently, finishing her sentence for her.

"You bet your boot-straps!"

"Thank you, my dear. Without you I know I would have lost the trail a long time ago." He gave her one of his wide, warm smiles and reached out to tousle her plumage.

"Just part of the service," she prowked delightedly.

All at once, her beak *thwaaaaaanged* up towards her eyes and locked in this uncomfortable position, which usually happened whenever she was feeling particularly pleased with herself.

"Er, Jm? Cd y fx m mndbl pls?"

"Certainly I can." With gentle force, he pushed her

beak down again until it was set properly. "That's better." She wiggled it back and forth. "I hate going wonky."

"Me too, Doris," said Cairo Jim meaningfully. "Me, too."

"Cairo Jim, Miss Doris," Euripides called, "look what the Wonder Camel has located."

Jim rose and Doris fluttered up and onto his outstretched arm. Together they made their way through the mess and destruction to join Euripides and Brenda.

For several minutes they all admired the ring and tried to work out the identity of the minuscule figures whose arms were reaching towards the heavens.

Then Jim glanced at his Cutterscrog Old Timers Archaeological Timepiece. "We're wasting time here. There's nothing we can do with all of this." He looked around his feet at the fallen mightiness. "We've got to get Bone!" He took out the Helena Hattbocks page from his shirt pocket. "Hmm," he hmmed after a moment. "Euripides, where is Samothraki?"

"Oh, it is an island in the north-east. Very remote. Hardly anyone goes there. Why, there's not even an aerodrome, as far as I know."

"Listen to this," said Jim. He cleared his throat of the dust and read steadily:

"Once the Tripod of Tiphistiades has been discovered, the legend calls for the collector of the Sacred Alabastron of Cronus and the altar and

the Tripod to venture forth to the island of Samothraki, or 'Samothrace' as it is sometimes known. There, at the ancient and long-disused site of the Sanctuary of the Great Gods, under the right conditions, the Divine Opening Ceremony can take place."

"Rerark," screeched Doris.

Euripides clicked his fingers. "You know, the Sanctuary of the Great Gods is a very mysterious place. Very strange. No one has yet been able to discover exactly what sort of worshipping took place there in ancient times. We *think* there was some sort of cult devoted to a great Mother Goddess, a goddess of Nature, but nobody knows for certain."

"A Mother Goddess?" squawked Doris. "Jim, it makes sense. Of course Bone's going there! You know how madly devoted he's always been to his *own* mother, Boadicea Tallulah Bone."

"Hmm." Jim folded the paper and returned it to his pocket. "You say there's no aerodrome, eh?" he asked in his old, confident tone.

"No." Euripides shook his curls. "Not according to what I have read of the place in my antiquities journals." He scratched his right kneecap. "We would have to ride north to Alexandroúpolis and catch a ferry to the island. It will take us at least a full night and day, even with Miss Brenda at full gallop."

The Wonder Camel gave a let's-hit-the-trail snort.

"Come on then, my lovely." Jim took Brenda's reins and started to lead her out of the destroyed Rotunda. "We've a long ride ahead of us."

"Here, Cairo Jim." Euripides scurried after them holding out the ring. "Why don't you wear this, until we get back to the Archaeological Museum in Athens? A finger would probably be the safest place for it, and *your* finger seems much more deserving than mine."

Jim paused and took the ring. "Thank you, Euripides. But only until we get it back to the Museum." He slid it onto the index finger of his left hand.

And a strange tingle passed inexplicably up his arm.

14

STIRRINGS FROM AFIELD

AT THE PRECISE MOMENT that Cairo Jim felt the strange tingle passing up his arm, other, *stranger* things were happening.

All around the world, in darkened Museums on the other side of the globe, in sun-drenched Art Galleries in countries close to Greece, in dust-free cabinets in private homes and mansions as far remote as New York and New Guinea, in dimly lit, box-filled rooms of Universities and Academies, in fact in all places where Greek antiquities were on carefully tended display or in semi-forgotten storage, there were *stirrings*.

These stirrings were so small, and they lasted for such a brief flicker of time, that they were almost undetectable:

A microscopic movement of marble in Manhattan.

A shushed shifting of statuary in Sydney.

A silent scraping in Seville.

A hushed heaving in Helsinki.

A little leaning in London.

A furtive fidget in Frankfurt.

An ant-like action in Athens.

A petite pulsation in Paris.

A twitch in Tokyo.

150

A rustle in Rangoon.

A blink in Berlin.

All of these stirrings happened at exactly the same second all around the world.

Then everything was still and silent.

15

REVELATIONS

THE HEADLIGHTS of Chief Inspector Reg Apollo's automobile swept across the forlorn and deserted mess that had been the Rotunda of Riákia.

As he climbed slowly from the driver's seat, he could not help thinking that the mess before him looked like the results of some giant's sudden and badly aimed sneeze, the explosion from which had scattered what had once been one of the architectural pinnacles of ancient civilization.

He shuddered, and forced himself to remember that an imagination was not part of an Antiquity Squad Chief Inspector's equipment. He shunted the image to one of the many back corners of his mind.

With early dusk hovering around him, and the silence clinging like an invisible swarm of insects, he began to walk through the piles of rubble. His black polished shoes nudged dusty fragments out of his path, and gradually his heart grew as heavily weighted as the fallen marble.

So weighted did his heart become that he almost missed seeing it: poking out from under a grotesquely broken slab, catching the thin light and seeming to glow from it, was an object that didn't belong here. A small piece of softness in all of this hard destruction.

Chief Inspector Reg Apollo bent down and fastened his delicate but strong fingers on the quill of the protruding gold-and-blue feather.

Carefully he pulled it from the rubble and he straightened himself again in the soft evening air. Studiously he moved it close to his eye.

With flared nostrils he took a discerning sniff of the soft edges.

A grim determination surged through his gritted teeth as he vowed to stop these destroyers, these vandals, these *plunderers*, at all costs.

While they were driving slowly northwards (with Herakles lumbering behind with the altar on one shoulder and the "heavy artillery" on the other), Neptune Bone told Desdemona more of his Master Plan.

"What?" croaked the bird. "Come again? Did you say there are *Titans* in that vase?"

"That's what I said, you foolish festermentation of follicles. And when we get to Samothraki, to a little site known as the Sanctuary of the Great Gods, I shall release them. Captain Neptune Flannelbottom Bone shall be the one to set them free."

"Why? What's in all this for you?"

The orange tassel on Bone's pumice-coloured fez billowed in the breeze. "Deification," he answered in a purring rumble.

"How rude," squawked Desdemona, screwing up her beak.

 153

"No, you doltish domain of density, I said deification."

Her red eyes throbbed curiously.

"It means," explained Bone with a contemptuous snort, "that when I release the Titans from the Sacred Alabastron of Cronus, I will become deified. I will become a god myself!"

There was a great hoarse cry as Desdemona sucked in a huge beakful of air. "You? A god? Is it possible?"

"Not only is it possible, Desdemona, it is also *inevitable*. In a very short time – hopefully by tomorrow night, in fact – we will be assembling all of the little bits and pieces we've collected. Then, at the stroke of midnight, which is the time Helena Hattbocks gave as the correct moment for the Divine Opening Ceremony to occur, we shall unleash the forgotten glories of the past – of that great neglectful superhighway of History – upon the uncaring modern world! Arrrrrrr!"

Desdemona's tongue was hanging out, and long, sticky streams of drool were joining her lower beak to the upholstery of the seat. She was so impressed that she couldn't even feel the fleas nipping at her underbelly (one of her most tender regions).

"And then," smirked Bone, "when I am indeed exalted, I shall have my way with the world."

The raven picked up her tongue with the endfeathers of her wings and stuffed it back into her gob. "What have you got planned, for instance?"

"Many things." He took a cigar from his waistcoat pocket and lit it with the Bugatti's built-in cigar-lighter. "The abolition of all those who disgust me; the destruction of the Old Relics Society and all who dwell within, especially that goody-two-boots wimp, Cairo Jim; the complete clearing of every centimetre of rainforested land – I have always found jungles to be sinister and unnecessary places; a Divine Edict whereby all gold, ivory, diamonds and the lesser jewels of the earth will instantaneously be offered to me; a Global Order for everyone to wear the fez and to spend four hours of every day on the maintenance and preservation of their fingernails; *the eradication of tofu*! A total restructuring of the world, in fact, so that it will run exactly as I desire it." He puffed indulgently, the smoke curling away behind him.

"How long's that going to take?"

"It won't happen overnight. After all, the world wasn't built in a day, you know. No, this Celestial and Divine Restructuring of the Planet Earth will take place over a long period of time. But that won't matter. I won't be growing old. Time will be my oyster."

"There's something you haven't thought of."

"Oh, yes? And what might that be, you insightful invoice of idiocy?"

"Them Titans you told me of. What about them? Suppose they don't like you getting all the glory, eh? Maybe *they'll* want to be the rulers?"

Bone threw back his head and laughed strongly until

his substantial belly wobbled against the steering-wheel. "No, no, no," he wheezed between laughs. "I *have* taken that into consideration. And I have made a contingency plan."

"Uh-huh?" She viewed him through slitted, throbbing eyes.

"Yes, Desdemona. I have absolutely no doubt that my Master Plan will not fit in at all with the ambitions of the Titans. After all, they will be itching to regain their former glory, won't they? I can't imagine that being scrunched up inside that bit of pottery for thousands of years will have made their desires any less. If I were them, I'd be keener than ever to take on my old stature once I'd been released."

"So? What'll you do?"

"It's simple. As soon as they have bestowed godliness upon my head, I shall tell them that I, their rescuer and fellow god, have Zeus and all his cohorts hidden in the bushes. That'll really get the Titans inflamed. It was Zeus, after all, who shoved them into the alabastron in the first place."

"But you haven't *got* Zeus and his cohorts." Suddenly she gulped. "Have you?"

"No, of course I haven't. But the Titans won't know that, not unless you tell them, and I don't think you'd do that, *would you*, Desdemona?"

"Nevermore, nevermore, nevermore!"

"So what will happen is this: I will inform the Titans that we can overpower the Olympians – Zeus and all those – by *surprise*. We must sneak up on them. Then when we're right on top of them, KAPOW!"

"But hang on. Didn't you tell me that the Titans are like giants?"

"Arrr. That I did."

"So, won't the Olympians see 'em coming?"

"They certainly will."

"So, if they see 'em coming…" Desdemona stopped and slapped her wings over her eyes. "Wait a minute, wait a minute, wait a minute. You haven't even *got* the Olympians!"

Bone sighed. "Let me explain the end of this plan, before your headfeathers burst and make a nasty mess all over my car. I will tell the Titans that, in order to have the advantage of surprise, we must approach the Olympians in the most unnoticeable way possible. Now, because of the low bushes where I will say the Olympians are gathered, and because of the immense height of the Titans, why, even if they crawled along the ground, the game would soon be given away. So I will suggest a different method of approach. I shall suggest" – and his voice dropped half an octave and his flabby lips moistened – "*that they get back inside the Sacred Alabastron of Cronus.* Then I shall say that I'll carry them to the bushes and, once we've come across the Olympians, the Titans can all pour out and have their way with them."

"Aha!" shrieked the bird.

"I will, of course, do no such thing. Once the Titans

are back inside the Sacred Alabastron of Cronus, I shall wedge the stopper in tighter than a blowfly's Adam's apple. And it won't come off again."

Desdemona let out a long whistle. "That's some plan. If I could, I'd take my feathers off to you, my Captain."

"That won't be necessary, although I do appreciate your admiration. It shows you have *some* common sense."

"So, what's the first thing you'll do after you've re-imprisoned the Titans, when you're Your Godliness?"

"Jocelyn Osgood," purred Bone.

"What?"

"I will whisk Jocelyn Osgood★ through time and space to be enthroned by my side. She shall become my goddess."

"Jocelyn Osgood? Of all the people on earth... She betrayed you years ago, for that Jim wimp... Why her?"

Bone took a long drag on the cigar and blew the smoke into Desdemona's face. "*Because she looks divine in jodhpurs,*" he replied. "It's about time she was given the chance to live up to her attired appearance."

"Bleccchh," spat the raven, who detested women even more than she detested men.

★The well-known Flight Attendant with Valkyrian Airways Limited, and "good friend" of Cairo Jim

The breeze changed direction, and Bone got a whiff of the unwashed feathers of his companion. He screwed up his nose. "Now leave me for a while, would you? Your propinquity distresses me. How is big boy faring?"

She squinted over her wing. "He's just plodding along, staring *stonily* ahead. Har-craark-har! Get it?"

"*You'll* get it if you don't pipe down," sneered Bone.

"I'll go where I'm appreciated," muttered Desdemona. She opened her wings and flew off to Herakles, who was still steadfastly following the Bugatti, his burdens shouldered silently.

He saw the black smudge of her body hovering in front of his face and, if his arms had not been otherwise engaged, he would have taken a mighty swipe at her. But all he could do was bear her presence and feel her croaking squawks vibrate off his marble skin.

"Boy oh boy, big old boy, you wouldn't believe what I just got a hearing-hole full of. That man's always said he's a genius, and maybe this time he's right."

Herakles plodded on.

"A god, that's what he'll be. And do you know what *I*'ll be, if I play me feathers right? If I'm very good to him? I'll tell you. I'll be a god, too. Crarrk! Although not as big a god as him, he wouldn't let that happen. No, I'll be more of a little god … what's that word? Yep, that's it – a *demi*-god. Desdemona the demi-god. But you can call me 'Demi'."

The strongest man in the world stared at her,

plodding all the while.

"Oh, I'll be so pious it'll make your marble crack. And guess what I'll be when I soar off into the sky? Give up? I'll tell you: Pious in the skyus! Ha ha ha ha ha!"

Then, with the moonlight pouring down onto them, Herakles kept plodding, further northwards in the dusty wake of the creeping automobile, while the raven began to teach him a song she had cobbled quickly together and which she had called "My Heart Belongs To Demi".

NORTH TO ALEXANDROÚPOLIS

With haste I race to Samothrace,
but not all on my own,
to boldly face the gross disgrace
that's Captain Neptune Bone...

Through the darkly-wrapped night galloped Brenda the Wonder Camel, her sturdy hoofs sometimes barely touching the ground beneath them. The rhythm of her pace spread through Cairo Jim's body and infiltrated his poetry cells, and the verse of their journey went round his head with a rapidly growing urgency.

Close to midnight, the archaeologist-poet was soothing Brenda's billowing mane with his handkerchief which he'd moistened with water from his water bottle, when a strange thought came to him. A thought that made some kind of eerie sense to him and to the pattern of the mess that Neptune Bone was trying to create. It all centred on a pen.

A few years back, he remembered, everyone had used fountain pens. Pens that you could refill with ink whenever they ran out, and that you could reuse for ever or until you lost them somewhere. Then a man named Biro had invented the world's first ballpoint writing pen.

Simple, made of plastic, and very affordable. So affordable, in fact, that when you had finished using it, you could just throw it away and buy another one. It was, thought Cairo Jim, the first fully disposable writing pen ever made.

When it had been introduced onto the market, Jim remembered how, for some strange reason that he couldn't explain to anyone at the time, he had felt a heavy, flat dread whenever he had seen the display cards full of the pens in the Gurna Stationery and Artificial Limbs Shoppe window. Tonight he understood *why* he had had that feeling.

The disposable society didn't start with Mr Biro! It started much longer ago, much further back in time. The ancient gods themselves introduced it to the world!

"Arrr," muttered Neptune Bone crankily. He gripped the steering wheel, his fingers pulsating with frustration, his pudgy knuckles almost bursting through his driving gloves. Raising a caterpillarian eyebrow, he glanced at the rear-vision mirror and saw Herakles plodding behind, with Desdemona perched on top of the shouldered altar.

The fez-wearing man had given up any idea of placing his foot heavily on the Bugatti's accelerator; he had tried that shortly after they had left the Rotunda of Riákia, and had driven for several minutes before realizing that Herakles had been left in a spiralling cloud of dust. Bone had had to turn the vehicle around and go back to meet him, otherwise the statue and all of the precious objects necessary for the Divine Opening Ceremony might end up anywhere.

He reached over with one hand to the seat next to him and tenderly fingered the box containing the Sacred Alabastron of Cronus. "Oh, for some speed," he said out loud. "If only big boyus back there could go a little faster, we'd be on that confounded ferry by now. This snail's pace is a disgrace to one so quick-witted such as myself is. Arrrr!"

The sun was starting to come up, but still the darkness was ruling the sphere of time. The Bugatti's headlights shone on a small road sign ahead.

"'Alexandroúpolis – one hundred and ninety-five kilometres,'" read Bone. His lips bloated into a scowl as he reached for a cigar.

As they crawled along in the shifting light, he made a mental note to himself that when he was truly Divine, he would also eliminate the whole concept of Slowness.

In the rear seat of the saddle, Doris had stopped her little game of trying to make Euripides yawn. It didn't seem to be working, even though she had been at it for the last two-and-a-half hours, constantly opening and closing her mandibles and shoving her face into his. All that had happened was that every time she had done it, he had smiled at her and commented on what a beautiful beak she had and how she reminded him, in some peculiar way, of his dear grandmother.

 **163**

Now he gave a big sigh (but not a yawn) and looked at her with sad eyes. "Ah, Miss Doris, this is a terrible business, is it not?"

"Rark," blinked the bird, happy to abandon her game before she got beak-cramps. "You bet your curly bits it is."

"As if the world has not already taken enough from my country," he said. "We have long been the victim of plunderers. Oh, yes, and not only in recent times. Do you know that the Roman emperor Nero took over six hundred beautiful statues from our Acropolis in Athens thousands of years ago?"

"The beast," Doris scowled. "Why?"

"Oh, because of their extraordinary beauty. And to show off to his people, I suppose. Now, many of those statues have completely disappeared. Vanished into the dusty drawers of Time."

"'Ah, that deceit should steal such gentle shapes,'" prowked Doris, quoting (almost) from *King Richard III*.

"It happened time and time again. Do you know, many of the things you saw back in the National Archaeological Museum in Athens were in fact reproductions? The originals can now only be seen in overseas museums, where they have more often than not been unjustly ensconced. And the site we are going to now, the Sanctuary of the Great Gods on Samothraki, why Miss Doris, there was once the most stunning statue ever carved presiding over that place."

"What was it?"

"It was the Winged Victory. Oh, she is huge, enormous, so big you would feel as inconsequential as an ant if you were to stand next to her. Like you, she has beautiful wings coming from her back, although her body is not that of a bird, but of a woman, with a rustling gown wrapped around her. She was – and still is – the most beautiful of all of the winged victories that once resided in ancient Greece. Our ancestors believed that, in the event of a war, she would bring victory to the Greeks, swiftly and surely. They had another name for her as well. It was 'Nike'."

"Where is she now?" Doris asked.

"Ah, last century she was taken from the Sanctuary of the Great Gods by some archaeologists who should have known better. The only place you can see her today is in the Louvre Museum in Paris, France. No longer does she watch over the Sanctuary."

Jim turned to Euripides. "Unfortunately, my friend, some of my colleagues from bygone days committed some dreadful acts. But not all of us are that way inclined."

Euripides's tired eyes glowed warmly. "I have never doubted your motivations for a second, Cairo Jim," he smiled.

"Nor have I," thought Brenda as the ground continued to blur underhoof and the sunlight began to dissolve the waning night's gloom.

▲ ▲ ▲

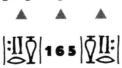

The further north they travelled, the cooler the air became. At a little after three o'clock in the afternoon, Brenda and her passengers approached the main road leading into the northern port city of Alexandroúpolis. Jim clicked his tongue and gave a gentle pull on her reigns and the Wonder Camel slowed her pace to a steady canter.

"You've done it, my lovely," congratulated Jim, patting the side of her neck. "You're a credit to the herd of the Wonder Camels of Thebes."

"Good one, Bren," squawked Doris, fluttering a wing across Brenda's left haunch.

"Quaaaaoooo!" Brenda fluttered her sweat-laden eyelashes and flared her heaving nostrils. It was always good to be appreciated.

"A most impressive display of efficiency and Bactrian charm," said Euripides. He ran his hand over his throat. "Oh, what I'd give for a cup of hot coffee with three marshmallows in it right now. My throat is quite perched."

Doris looked at him quizzically.

"I mean, *parched*."

"Yes," Jim nodded. "We could all do with a little refreshment before we get to the wharf. Look, my lovely, up ahead. See that refreshment shop?"

"Quaoo."

"Let's head there. We'll whet our whistles and then be off to the ferry."

It was an idea that suited everybody.

Five minutes later, Brenda was slurping from a huge bucket of chilled water while Doris sat on Jim's shoulder, sharing with him (by way of two drinking straws) a large paper cup of home-made lemonade. Euripides was resting on a chair in front of the shop, balancing on his knee a cup of hot coffee with some marshmallows floating, and gradually melting, in it. He was waiting for the exact second when the marshmallows would submerge, as this was the best time to take the very first sip of the coffee, and he savoured such moments almost as much as the moments he spent looking at the antiquities in his Gallery of Forgotten Gods.

While he was patiently waiting for the moment to arrive, his eye caught on a poster that had been nailed onto a nearby telegraph pole. His eye narrowed, and widened, and narrowed again as he read the information on the poster. Then the dusty curls on his head had a little quiver, and he said, "Oh, dear me."

Jim took his mouth from the straw. "What's wrong, Euripides?"

"Cairo Jim, you'd better have a look at this. Quickly!" He stood, being careful not to spill his coffee, and went to the telegraph pole.

Jim and Doris followed.

"Reerraarrrrk!" screeched the macaw. "What in the name of Amenophis is this?"

Jim removed his cracked desert sun-spectacles and read out loud the words on the poster:

<u>WANTED</u>

FOR THEFT OF PRICELESS ARCHAEOLOGICAL ANTIQUITIES FROM THE DELPHI MUSEUM, THE ROTUNDA OF RIÁKIA, AND OTHER POSSIBLE SITES:

CAIRO JIM. Archaeologist (professional), poet (non-professional). Member, Old Relics Society, Cairo, Egypt. Frequent pith helmet & special desert sun-spectacles wearer. Sometimes also known as "Jim of Cairo".

DORIS. Macaw (professional). Feathers: blue and gold, lots of them. Habitual squawker, often screeches. No known aliases.

BRENDA THE WONDER CAMEL. Camel (professional). Eyelashes: notable. Prolific snorter. Nice hoofs. No known aliases.

MAN. Identity unknown. Dressed in blue suit without necktie. Abundant, neatly arranged curls on top of head. Gentlemanly walk.

Any information regarding the whereabouts of these suspected felons must be reported immediately to the nearest branch of the Antiquities Squad. A reward will be paid handsomely.

AUTHORISED BY CHIEF INSPECTOR
REG APOLLO OF THE HELLENIC BRANCH OF
THE ANTIQUITIES SQUAD

"Suspected felons?" spluttered Doris, her wings flapping against Jim's face and neck. "What outrage is this in the world of men?"

"Well, swoggle me laterally with a lawsuit," gasped Cairo Jim. "Talk about getting hold of the wrong end of the papyrus!"

"I am a fugitive!" exclaimed Euripides, dropping his cup of by now drinkable coffee onto the ground and putting his hands to his face. "I *knew* I shouldn't have accompanied you lot on this trip!" He moved his hands up to the top of his head and began trying to flatten out his curls before anyone noticed his distinctive hairstyle. "I should have stayed put in my safe little Gallery, where these kinds of mistakes could *never* happen!"

"Quaaooo?" Brenda had lumbered silently over to them to see what all the fuss was about.

"This Apollo character must be following us," said Jim. "He's obviously been too late to catch Bone in the act, but he must have seen us each time."

"Rark! What do we do now?"

"There's no time to waste," announced the archaeologist-poet, quickly removing his pith helmet and tucking it under one of the flaps on Brenda's saddlebags. "We have to get straight down to the docks and on to the first available ferry to Samothraki. Hopefully we won't have to wait for too long until one sails." He looked at Euripides. "You, my friend, are probably the least recognizable of all of us, on account of the hazy description of you on this poster. I dare say there'll be lots of these notices plastered all over town. We'll need you to purchase our ferry tickets for us … you can leave your coat in one of Brenda's saddlebags. While you're getting the tickets, we'll find a shadowy corner to lurk about in."

"Hmph!" hmphed Doris. "To think – *us*, lurking in shadowy corners!"

"I understand," nodded Euripides, taking off his jacket and stowing it where Jim had suggested.

"Whatever you do," said Jim, "say as little to anyone as possible. Don't start any conversations that might give us all away."

"My lips will be walrussed."

They all looked at Euripides quizzically. "I mean, *sealed*."

"Good man," said Jim. "Now, Doris, my dear, listen carefully: it's of the utmost importance that you keep your beak low for the time to come. You must be as small and unnoticeable as you can."

"Rerk," nodded the macaw, blinking her tiny dark eyes.

"But what about Miss Brenda?" inquired Euripides. "She will not be easy to keep out of the public eye, surely? After all, there are not too many Wonder Camels up here in the north of Greece."

"Don't worry," Jim said, stroking Brenda's mane. "I'll think of something. I have before, haven't I, my lovely?"

"Quaaooo." She rolled her head in a circle, and the

ring on Jim's finger – the one that had been found at the Rotunda of Riákia – glinted for a second in the sunlight.

"Ha," he said. "'Only One Kind of Man Will Bring You Good Fortune When You Seek The Forgotten.'" He took a last look at the name of the Antiquities Squad Member at the bottom of the Wanted poster. "I don't think our Chief Inspector Apollo's *that* kind of man, do you? Come on, let's get moving!"

A SHADOWY PASSAGE

LUCK APPEARED, for the time being at least, to be leaning towards them.

Down at the port, Euripides soon found out that the daily ferry to Samothraki was due to depart in thirty-six minutes precisely. He quickly purchased two gentlemen's tickets, and, having made sure that he was not being watched, scuttled (in an elegant sort of way) over to the shadowy corner of the wharf where Jim, Doris and Brenda were secreted behind some enormous baskets of prickly pears which were on their way from Corinth to the northern regions.

"Thirty-six minutes, eh?" said Jim.

"Precisely," said Euripides.

"Rark!" Doris gave a quiet (for once) screech and raised her wings momentarily above her head. "At least we won't have to skulk over here for too long, then."

"Quaooo," Brenda snorted timidly.

"Cairo Jim, have you yet determined how we are to get Miss Brenda onto the ferry without raising any suspicious eyebrows?"

"As a matter of fact, Euripides, we have. Watch this. Doris, if you wouldn't mind giving me a helping wing?"

"My pleasure," she squawked.

Then, for the next few minutes, Cairo Jim and Doris used all of their expertise and resourcefulness – not to mention a good dash of creativity – to transform Brenda the Wonder Camel into what appeared to be a substantial bundle of luggage owned by the Turkish Women's Championship Tent Erection Team, complete with luggage labels bearing the appropriate information.

"It is a grand thing that we live in an era of ceaseless possibilities," reflected Jim as he put the finishing touches to the disguise, in the form of a big knotted bow of rope on the top of Brenda's rear, and camouflaged, hump.

"It certainly is," nodded Euripides.

"All we need do now is march down the gangway when the time to board is announced. By designing Brenda's camouflage so it almost reaches the ground, we can push her gently so it appears that we're sliding the luggage of the Turkish Women's Championship Tent Erection Team along. Just walk *smoothly*, Brenda."

"Quaaooo!"

"During the voyage—how long will it take, Euripides?"

"About two-and-a-half hours, so they told me."

"Good," Jim said. "During the voyage we'll all stay below in the hold, with the automobiles and carts and other vehicles of necessity. I'm afraid we couldn't risk being seen on deck, or in any of the passenger lounges."

"That's for sure," Doris blinked.

"Of course," Euripides agreed.

 173

"Quaooo," came a slightly muffled snort from the nostril holes of the luggage of the Turkish Women's Championship Tent Erection Team. Jim patted it reassuringly, and several of the luggage labels appeared to flutter.

While they had been so engaged, none of them had heard the noise of a particularly large and dusty Bugatti, or the clunking sounds – sounds that seemed like footsteps – of a heavily draped and strangely hulking object, as they all moved across the wharf and into the hold of the ship.

The small but sturdy ferry *The Spirit of Nike* set sail only a little after its advertised departure schedule, and soon the vessel had left the port of Alexandroúpolis and was being gently rolled and lifted by the wider waters, where the northern Mediterranean Sea gradually ran into the Sea of Marmara.

Down in the cargo hold, in a gloomy corner at the back of the hollow cavern, behind the dozens of "vehicles of necessity" that had been parked carefully by their owners prior to sailing time, the small band of Jim, Doris, Euripides and the luggage of the Turkish Women's Championship Tent Erection Team huddled in carefully guarded quietness.

"I think," Jim whispered to them all after the ferry had entered the choppier waters, "that when we've berthed at Samothraki we should remain here until all the vehicles and things have been driven away by their owners. Docks get fairly deserted after the cargo's been unloaded, and that'd be the best time to make our move."

"Rerark! Good thinking, Jim."

"Thank you, my dear. In the meantime, let's get some shut eye. What do you say, Brenda, my lovely?"

But the only sound to emerge from the exhausted bundlings beside him was a gentle snort of a snore.

Above and slightly to the left, in the smoky, lurching First Class Lounge, Captain Neptune Bone had invaded the only decent armchair, and was sprawled inelegantly in it, haughtily surveying his fellow passengers through his superior eyes.

After a few minutes of this watchful activity, and after many puffs on his foul-smelling cigar, he adjusted his latest fez (a jacaranda-coloured number with a soft, wattle-yellow tassel) and turned to Desdemona, who was sitting by the armchair, trying to peck away the fleas from her netherfeathers.

"Are you absolutely positive that you tied that tarpaulin securely around Big Boy?"

"Crark, you betcha. It gave me quillsful of pleasure doing that. He's a brute, he is." Her eyeballs throbbed redly as she continued her attack on her resident nuisances.

"And you tied one end of the rope to the Bugatti, like I told you to?"

"Yep. Right around the back axle. Don't worry, he can't get up to any marbleised mischief down there."

"Arrr." Bone took another puff on the cigar, and patted the Sacred Alabastron of Cronus box that was resting on the paunch of his waistcoat. "Not long to go now, bird. Not long at all."

Desdemona stopped her pecking and hopped up onto the arm of the chair. "My Captain, it's time we squawked."

"I beg your pardon?" He blew a shaft of smoke into her face.

"Ergh! I mean, I'll squawk and you talk."

"What could I possibly desire to talk to you about? No, Desdemona, leave me to be alone with my last few hours of mortality. This is a time for human introspection, and there are many things I wish to dwell upon—"

"CRAAAAAAAAARRRRRRK!"

The sound was as deafening as a gunshot, and was uttered as close to Bone's ear as she could get her beak. The large man's eyes shot open as wide as saucers, and his ears went moth-silent, then alarm-ringing, then moth-silent again. Then they quivered before his hearing returned to a close version of being normal.

"I think, my Captain, that you should listen to me."

"You grottily garrulous gimcrack!"

She opened her beak again, wide and threatening, but he spoke quickly. "All right, all right, all right, but make it snappy! My time is precious."

"I know that. Don't worry, I'll be brief. It occurs to me, Neptune Flannelbottom Bone, that, because I have been your faithful and constant companion throughout many of your recent years, and because I have provided you with the comfort of friendship, entertainment and the unparalleled pleasure of my company—"

"Get on with it! Arrrr!"

"That, because of all of these factors, you would want to give me a little something when you have achieved your exalted state. A little reward, you might call it. For being so sweet to you." She tried to flutter her eyelashes, but they had long ago been singed away by the ashings from Bone's cigars, and the effect looked more like an old-fashioned film flickering out of the projector and all around her eyefeather region.

"A reward, eh?"

"A reward." She stopped her flickering and her eyes throbbed expectantly.

Bone squirmed and carefully managed to cross his legs. "And what," he said, tugging down the hem of his plus-fours to his kneecap, "might you have in mind?"

"What you said before. Defecation."

Bone arched an eyebrow.

"I mean, desecration."

He arched his eyebrow higher.

Desdemona snapped her beak open and shut. "No, degradation."

His eyebrow was now almost meeting his hairline.

"Oh, you know what I mean!" she spat.

"You don't mean *deification*, surely, Desdemona?"

"Crark, yep, that's it. Yep, by the poet Poe, that's

what I want." She hopped across to the other arm of the chair. "Oh, go on, Captain, I deserve it, don't I? For all the tears I shed for you when you got lost under the Red Sea, for all the times I let you stub out your cigar on my noggin, for all those – *bleccchhh* – envelopes I licked for you. Please, please, please, with seaweed on?"

He looked at her silently for a few long minutes. His eyes glazed and then cleared and then glazed again, and the smoke from his cigar curled up through his beard and into his hairy nostrils. Then he reached out and put his index finger firmly on the top of her beak.

"Arrr. Yes, you cranky carrion, you *have* been at my esteemed side through many moments of greatness. And it should follow that, because of your close proximity over such a long time, some of my subtle glory should have rubbed off onto yourself. Although where it shows on you, I have no idea. But–" he puffed the cigar – "I have been a magnanimous human being, and so, as one of my last acts in this incarnation, I shall promise you your reward."

"Oh, Captain, thank you, thank you, thank you. Just a little deifacet … dayadef … I only want to be a *little* god … a demi-god, if you please."

"Oh, you shall be a *very* little god, Desdemona. But a very special one, nonetheless."

"Special? And what will I be god of?" she croaked hoarsely. "Something of great importance to humanity?"

"Oh, yes. Something absolutely vital to the human

race. Something that humans will always need in this world, to keep them in line."

"What's that?" she drooled. "Wisdom? Beauty? Cleverness?"

"No. Something with which you are *well* acquainted."

She thought for a moment, running her yellow tongue around the edges of her beak. "I know, I know! It's seaweed, isn't it? Me, Desdemona the Goddess of Seaweed!"

"No, it's not seaweed."

"Then what?"

His eyes lit up as he moved his fingers to her neckfeathers and closed them gently around her throat. "*Vermin!*" he purred. "*Aaaarrrrrr!*"

"*CRAAARRRRRRRRRKKKKK!*"

Above and all around, the clouds were billowing and congregating, as though they had all been called together by some unknown Gatherer. Silently they swirled, slowly and wispily, through the heavens – from the west and the south and the east, from points far-scattered around the globe.

The moon was already full in the darkening sky; its beams tumbled down onto the ferry as it neared the coastline of the egg-shaped island of Samothraki. The moonlight seemed to catch the crest of each wave of the ocean, and infuse it with a brilliant white glow. The linings of the clouds were also glowing, and gradually, here and there, barely visible against the darkness,

 179

strange objects that did not belong in the air but were there anyway were also being bathed in the celestial glow. They also moved silently, these strange objects, through the quietly turbulent sky, as if they were riding on the very clouds themselves.

NIGHT BEFORE BATTLE

"CAARRAAARRK! What was that bump?"

"Steady on, Soon-to-be-Goddess of Vermin, don't get your feathers in a fluster. It was merely the ferry making contact with our dock. This should be the port town of Kamariotisa."

"We've arrived?"

"If you were able to read, I'd spell it out for you. Yes, we are here. At the island that will soon become the destination for countless pilgrims. Arrrrr."

"What're we waiting for, then? Let's get downstairs and get that car outta here, with Big Boy and all!"

"There's no hurry. We still have six or so hours until midnight. It shan't take us more than an hour to get to the Sanctuary of the Great Gods, even with Herakles and his snail's pace. We shall sit back here for a while, and allow all of the mortals to depart."

"If you say so. Ouch! Drat these fleas!"

"And, in the meantime, you can put that tongue of yours to good use. My spats are *filthy*."

Chief Inspector Reg Apollo, who had been sitting less than a stone's throw from Neptune Bone – but in the Second Class Passenger Lounge, and therefore totally

unaware of his presence – was one of the first passengers to reach his automobile in the hold.

As soon as the huge door opened, he started the engine and, with the dozens of other vehicles, proceeded in a slow manner down the gangway and onto the dock.

He drove into the main street of Kamariotisa and parked the car at a small place overlooking the ocean, near where some fishermen and women were slapping octopus against the rocks to tenderize it. Reaching into the glovebox, he took out a small electronic device which he deftly plugged into the cigarette-lighter socket on the dashboard. Attached to this device was a set of earphones which he put on his head, adjusting both canisters until they were comfortable on his ears.

With a twiddle of the wireless control buttons, he was at last able to pick up the high-frequency Morse Code signals that were being sent to him from the Head Office of the Antiquities Squad Hellenic Branch Office in Athens:

BE BE BE – BEEP – BE BEEP – BEEP BE –
BEEP BE BE
BEEP BE BE BE – BEEP BE BEEP BEEP
BE BE BEEP BE – BEEP BEEP BEEP – BE
BEEP BE
BE BEEP – BEEP BE –BEEP BE – BEEP
BEEP BEEP – BE BE BEEP – BEEP BE –
BEEP BE BEEP BE – BE – BEEP BEEP –
BE – BEEP BE – BEEP BE – BEEP!

Reg Apollo listened closely. Each urgent beep of sound was like a thousand needles pricking into the silence. Each urgent beep built up the news about the thousands of Greek antiquities that had been discovered to have vanished within the last twenty-four hours from all around the world.

His lips became heavy with grimness. "By Zeus," he silently wondered, "how are they managing a crime such as *this*?"

At last Neptune Bone and Desdemona sauntered down to the hold, he clutching the Sacred Alabastron of Cronus box tightly to his over-expanded chest, she perched smugly on top of his fez.

They got into the Bugatti and started the engine. With a smooth gliding motion, the car moved off the ferry and onto the dock, accompanied by what sounded like heavy, clunking footsteps echoing in the tinny hollow of the cargo hold. Soon the noises had faded into the evening's distance.

Over in their gloomy corner, Doris stretched her wings and blinked impatiently. "Rerk! I didn't think that last one was ever going to leave." She hopped up onto an empty packing case and peered over the top.

"How is it?" whispered Jim.

"The coast is clear. Or at least the hold is. I'll let you know about the *coast* when we're off the ferry."

"Very amusing," said Euripides.

The luggage of the Turkish Women's Championship

Tent Erection Team snorted urgently. "Come on," came the telepathic thought, "there's no time to waste."

"Come on," urged Jim, rising to his feet and smoothing down his shorts, "there's no time to waste." He helped the bundle of luggage to its hoofs. "Don't worry, my lovely, as soon as we're away from the docks you'll be a Wonder Camel once again. Euripides?"

"Yes, Cairo Jim?"

"I think it'd be a good idea if you were to venture out first and see if you can buy a map of the island. Somewhere on the dock there'll probably be a little booth selling small items; there usually is on islands such as this."

"Rightio, yes, a good idea it surely is." He smeared down his curls as best he could and, with a nervous wink, crept silently out of the hold.

Luckily for Jim, Doris and Brenda the Wonder Luggage, there was no one around to see their curious exit from the vessel.

The Bugatti of Bone and the raven followed the main road to the small coastal town of Paleopolis, which was the closest settlement to the Sanctuary of the Great Gods. Even though Bone was bold to take such an open route, he was, of course, unable to speed boldly along it, for the pace of Herakles (still carrying the humungous objects on his shoulders) slowed him down considerably.

Cairo Jim, on the other hand, could not afford to be

bold. Because of their fugitive status, he, Doris, Euripides and Brenda quickly left the town of Kamariotisa under cover of the night, and, following the map of Samothraki which Euripides had bought, proceeded along a roughly paved road that led up towards the mountains, and to a small village called Chora.

When they were safely out of Kamariotisa, they removed Brenda's disguise (much to her relief – she had discovered that the old saying "All dressed up with nowhere to go" was quite true, as she had been starting to *feel* like a bundle of luggage and had been wondering for the last hour or so exactly where she was going to be freighted).

Cairo Jim took his pockmarked pith helmet from Brenda's saddlebag and put it on. "I don't feel quite prepared without it," he explained to his friends.

After half an hour they reached Chora. The only light that greeted them – apart from the strong moonlight – was from a series of tiny fairy-lights that had been strung across the narrow, steeply rising laneways. Brenda's hoofs clopped loudly on the cobbled stones. All of the windows in the old, old houses were either in darkness or boarded up by shutters.

"Good," whispered Jim. "It appears that everyone's retired for the night." He looked up towards the top of the town, to a huge, black mass that rose behind the topmost houses into the cloud-laden sky.

"Rark," Doris squawked quietly. "What is it, Jim? A mountain?"

"Ah," said Euripides, "that will be Mount Fengari. It is the highest mountain around these parts. As you know, I'm not one for legends, but it is said that the great god Poseidon actually watched the Trojan War from those very peaks."

"It seems the gods are all around us," blinked Doris.

"That it does, my dear," whispered Jim urgently. "And we'd better make tracks if we're going to do something about it." He nudged Brenda forward, and they all ascended towards the mountain.

"The trail we want is up there," Jim said in a determined voice.

At the top of the town, in a fold of Mount Fengari, they came to an old, abandoned castle. Jim pulled Brenda to a halt and took out his compass, torch and the map from his knapsack.

"Here, my dear," he said to Doris, putting the torch under her wing. "Please illuminate us."

"Rark. My light is your light." She turned it on and lit up the map.

"Which way?" asked Euripides.

Looking at the compass and the map, Jim gave a nod. "Due north," he announced. "Only a couple of kilometres or so."

Doris swung the torch's beam around. The yellowy light passed across dark, hulking stands of trees set on top of the hills and crags. Then she gave a squawk. "Reerraark! Look, over there!"

They all peered in the direction she was illuminating, and (thanks also to the strong moonlight) they saw a wide dirt track leading down the steep hillside.

Jim checked the compass once again. "You clever bird. That's our track all right."

"It looks like it snakes off into the wilderness," murmured Euripides. "There do not appear to be any houses or dwellings down there at all."

"That's because there aren't," Jim said. "Come on, my lovely, there's the trail we need to hit."

"Quaaaooo!"

Slowly they made their way, bathed by the moonlight and by the faint dew that was falling from above. So concerned were they with keeping their eyes on the curving, rock-strewn dirt track, they did not notice the myriad of strange objects congregating far above, amidst the heavy, swirling clouds in the skies.

"Rark!" Doris exclaimed at one point, when Brenda had rounded a bend and was descending into a small ravine. "Listen. What on earth is that noise?"

"Whoa for a moment, my lovely."

Brenda stopped and pricked up her Wonder Camel ears.

"I hear it," whispered Euripides.

"So can I," Jim looked around.

Clang-clang. It was very faint.

"Bells?" asked Euripides.

"Gee up, my lovely."

Brenda started off, slowly.

Clang-clang. Clang-clang. Clang-clang. Clang-clang-clang-clang-clang!

The sounds were all around them now, tinny and echoing, some of them coming from very close to the edge of the dirt track, others ringing faintly from hillsides far away.

Clang-clang-clang-clang-clang. Clang-clang. Clang-clang. Clang-clang. Clang-clang. Clang-clang!

Doris turned on the torch and directed the beam into the low, black bushes and the silhouettes of the stunted trees by the track's edge.

She gave a shattering screech. "*REEEEEERRRR-RAAAAARRRRK*!"

Dozens and dozens of tiny, lemon-coloured eyes were staring unblinkingly at them. Still, the clanging continued.

Clang-clang-clang-clang-clang.

Some of the eyes were close to the darkened ground; some of them were at about knee-height, while others seemed to be looking down from the tops of the short trees.

Brenda snorted in terror. "Quaaaaaooooooo!"

"Steady on, my lovely," Jim frantically patted the side of her great neck, "nothing to be alarmed about."

"Hundreds of small, lemon-coloured eyes staring at you in the middle of the night?" thought Brenda. "You call *that* nothing to be alarmed about?"

"Goats," said Euripides.

"Raark? Goats?"

"Yes. They are only goats. Many Greek islands have more goats on them than human beings. Samothraki is one of them."

"Well, swoggle me perpendicularly," breathed Cairo Jim.

Doris moved the torchlight more slowly. Here and there, little bits of goats emerged in the shimmer: some hoofs gambolling away; the glint of old, tarnished brass as a goat-bell swung back and forth; the odd beard below chewing, teethy jaws; a black or cream-coloured ear amidst the leafy growth of the small trees.

"They're even in the trees!" she exclaimed.

"Ah, yes. I have read of them in my journals. They are the famous Samothrakian Tree-Climbing Goats, you know."

"Now *there's* a skill you don't read much about these days," pondered Cairo Jim, urging Brenda forward.

After nearly an hour, the dirt track veered off to the right, and became narrower and rougher with many more loose stones.

Brenda opened her nostrils wide and took such a deep sniff that both Jim and Euripides felt the trillerie of air as it passed deep inside her.

"Brenda's discovered something, haven't you, my lovely?"

"Quaaooo!" She took another deep sniff.

"I know, I know," cried Doris, fluttering about on

Jim's pith helmet. "It's the ocean. You've smelt the sea, haven't you, Bren?"

She rolled her head in a huge circular movement.

At the end of this new track they saw the crests of small ocean waves glinting as each captured the moon and let it go again.

Jim fumbled around in his knapsack for a moment and then withdrew his binoculars. Putting them to his eyes, he looked ahead, moving his vision to the right and the left, and squinting hard. Then he noticed something.

"The Sanctuary of the Great Gods," he whispered in a voice filled with awe and foreboding, rippling with admiration for the ancient architects and weighted by dread for what might happen in a few short hours. "The very place itself."

Nestled in a small valley close to the ocean lay the entire complex of the Sanctuary. In the centre of the site, the moonlight picked out five columns – the only five columns anywhere around that appeared still to be standing – on top of which sat a lone, forlorn piece of stone architrave. Many broken columns lay on their sides, slumped against the outer slopes of the small valley; resting in the places where they had ended up after they had been dislodged and had rolled away.

To the northern end, the foundations of a large, circular building were visible. Near this, Jim could just make out, by adjusting the focus on the binoculars, the remnants of a tiny amphitheatre. Occasionally the night's beams shone down on a piece of statuary: a damaged head lying cheekdown against the grass, or a sculpted torso still standing on a weathered marble pedestal.

At a little site at the western perimeter of the Sanctuary, many headstones had been erected, some of them still standing amongst the ancient, tall grasses, others cracked, shattered and sprawling all over the place.

"That must be the necropolis," the archaeologist-poet said. He handed the binoculars to Doris. "Here, my dear, see if you can spy Bone anywhere about."

While she was doing this, Euripides pointed out the shadow of Mount Fengari behind them. "Do you see how there is the mountain at that end of the Sanctuary of the Great Gods, and the ocean at the other? It was the same with many of the ancient sites on islands such as this. They used to have an enormous temple to Zeus at the mountain end, and another to Poseidon at the ocean end." He sighed sadly. "They are gone, also…"

"Rerk! Nope. No sign of that demented fashion victim trapped by time."

"He'll be down there somewhere, all right." Jim looked at his Cutterscrog Old Timers Archaeological Timepiece. "Speaking of time, it's nearly nine o'clock. Three hours until Bone tries it on. I suggest we all head down to the Sanctuary and find a secluded spot there where we can get some shuteye for a few hours. Brenda was the only one who slept on the ferry – and no wonder, after her Herculean effort at getting us all the way up to Alexandroúpolis – and I think we should be as refreshed and as alert as possible if we're to thwart Bone to the utmost degree."

They all agreed with him, and, as he directed Brenda quietly down the smaller trail, he couldn't help wondering, with a lump in his throat, what the utmost degree would be for this evening, an evening that Humanity would have to wrestle with.

And win.

19

THE NIGHT CONTINUES

A SECLUDED CORNER was soon found, just outside the boundary of the Sanctuary – Jim felt that it wouldn't be quite right to camp *within* such a once-holy, and still important, site.

Under a wide, gnarled plane tree, in a boulder-strewn glade surrounded by thick and windswept shrubs, they settled themselves for the next few hours. Jim unsaddled Brenda and set her saddle against one of the larger boulders. He and Euripides fashioned themselves makeshift pillows out of their luggage and clothing, and propped themselves up on either side of the saddle's ornate macramé covering. Doris fluttered up to one of the lower branches of the plane tree, and found a comfortable claw-hold to use as her perch.

Then, despite the growing trepidation that was coursing through their insides, they all gave in to their exhaustion, and slept.

All of them, that is, except the Wonder Camel. She had slept quite enough on the ferry (Wonder Camels only require a small amount of sleep to keep them energetic, no matter how much exertion they have been through) and was now wide awake. She stood at one end of the glade, keeping a silent, vigilant eye on her

friends, her ears alert for any signs of intrusion.

She heard the sounds of a distant brook, gurgling away over time-worn-smooth rocks and pebbles.

She listened to the *clang-clang-clang* of the army of goats' bells in the hills above.

She felt the dew settling on the grasses and the boulders and in her long, long eyelashes.

She watched her feathered friend who was muttering in her sleep on her branch-perch. "Rark ... 'as glorious to this night ... as is a winged messenger of heaven' ... rark." (Even in her sleep, thought Brenda, she still quotes from Shakespeare.)

The Wonder Camel lowered her head and chomped on a tall tuft of grass. When she looked up again, she noticed the thin, singular shaft of purest moonlight that had managed to spear down through the thick leaves of the plane tree. This bright shaft had come to rest on the ring from the Rotunda of Riákia, now on Cairo Jim's finger, and the tiny figures on the ring were bathed in a cool, almost pulsating glow.

"Quaaooo!" she snorted quietly. She looked across to the ground on the other side of her saddle, to where Euripides was snoring. With every exhalation he made, his curls gave a little quiver, almost like a jig of sleepiness.

For a long time, Brenda kept watch over everything.

She lowered her head to take another chomp on the grass, when a curious noise, close by, in the shrubbery undergrowth, froze her jaw mid-bite.

Holding her head rigid, she listened with all her

incredible powers for the noise to come again. Her carefully measured Wonder Camel hearing began to sort out the sounds she already knew, the sounds she had heard previously and which were not this new, curious noise:

Clang-clang-clang-clang. No, it wasn't the goats' bells.

Nor was it the infinitesimal *plops* of the settling dew.

It wasn't the *shush*edness of the tiny breezes that played around her ears.

Or the silky *ssss*ing of the leaves overhead.

She waited patiently and then, when she was about to scrape a hoof against the ground, the curious noise came back:

Clop-clop-clop. P-b-h-oooo. Clop-clop. P-b-hoo.

This time Brenda got a good earful of it. She turned her head to the direction from where it had come. Behind the bushes, she thought she saw a movement.

Lifting her hoofs very carefully, she lumbered almost invisibly towards the bushes. Once there, she parted them gently with her snout.

Clop-clop-clop. P-b-h-oooo. P-b-hoo. Clop-clop-clip-clop.

There, in a small clearing, alone and foraging, stood an odd creature. A creature that Brenda had never seen in the world before.

The Wonder Camel blinked her heavy eyelashes at it and stared for some time. What *was* this thing?

At first, when she had beheld its bearded face and well-developed human chest and strong forearms and clearly-defined hands, she had thought it was a man.

But now, as she gazed further down the creature's body, she knew it couldn't possibly be. For below the waist, the creature resembled a distant cousin of hers: a horse!

The creature continued to move about the clearing, plucking small handfuls of berries from off the bushes and eating them delicately. Every so often his tail swished back and forth and he used a fine finger to smooth down his beard.

Then Brenda remembered something: when, as an inquisitive calf, she had eaten all of those *Encyclopaedia Britannica*s (the information from which had never left her system), she had come across a picture of a creature such as this, under the Mythological Beings section. The creature was a Centaur.

She stood looking at it for a long time. "They said you'd disappeared thousands of years ago," she thought. "But of course you're still here. *Just because they all stopped believing in you doesn't mean you stopped existing.* I understand that."

Her thought had travelled, and now the Centaur looked up from his berries and saw Brenda gazing at him through the bushes. He received her thought and nodded his head slowly.

"Quaaooo," snorted Brenda.

The Centaur raised his arm to her and lowered it. All at once, there was a mighty, rocketing explosion of sound from the plane tree behind Brenda. The Centaur looked up, his eyes filled with terror. Swiftly he turned and, picking up his hoofs, galloped heavily off into the tree-covered mountainside.

"*REEEEEEERRRRRRRRAAAAAAAAAAAAA
AARRRRRRRRRRRRRKKKKK! REEEEEEEEEE
EEEEEEEEKKKKKKK! RAAAAAAAAAARRRAA
AARR RAAARRK!*"

Brenda had only heard that sort of screech once
before, but there was no doubt at all in her mind: her
friend Doris was in grave danger.

20

THE STAGE IS SET

CHIEF INSPECTOR REG APOLLO, dozing on the front seat of his Antiquities Squad vehicle at the eastern side of the Sanctuary, was jerked awake by the screech of terror.

Jim and Euripides both heard it at the same time – it ricocheted down from the leaves of the tree above them. They sat bolt upright as the screech faded away over the treetops.

Brenda shot about-face and charged towards the secluded corner of their makeshift camp. She arrived with a loud smattering of hoofs.

"Brenda, my lovely," blurted Cairo Jim, now on his feet and looking worried. "It's Doris, have you seen her?"

"Quaaaaoooo!" She snorted in the negative.

"She's not up there," muttered Euripides, shining the torch into the plane tree's boughs.

"Something's got her. She's been feathernapped." The archaeologist-poet gently grabbed hold of Brenda's mane and hoisted himself up onto her bare fore hump. "Are you coming, Euripides?"

"But what about the saddle?" Euripides bit his lip and in the next instant said, without hesitation, "Yes, of course. I am with you always."

Jim offered his hand, and Euripides pulled himself up to Brenda's nether hump. "Sniff her out, my lovely," cried Jim as the Wonder Camel headed off lurchingly into the dark undergrowth.

"Crark! One squawk outta you and your feathers'll be history! Ha ha ha ha ha."

"Lay off, you fleabag felon," Doris spat. She squirmed under the weight of the fragments of statues that Desdemona had rolled onto her wings.

"Nevermore, nevermore, nevermore!"

"Rerk! I know we've never seen beak to beak on much, but what have I ever done to you?" Doris tried again to tug her wing from under the heavy marble arm on top of it, but it was no use. "Why all this brutishness?"

Desdemona lay on her side, in the long grass of the necropolis, facing Doris. She propped her head and beak in the palmfeathers of her wing and picked off a flea from her belly. "Oh, pardon me," she rasped snidely. "All this 'brutishness'? Why, forgive me, for I am merely a grotty raven. Unlike the noble and gaudy macaw, 'brutishness' comes natural to the likes of myself." She crushed the flea and flicked it at the nearest gravestone.

"Let me go!"

"All in good time, have no fear. Ha ha ha ha ha!"

Doris thrashed her head from side to side. "What do you want with me?" she squawked.

"Oh, that's easy." Her eyeballs throbbed redder than ever as she leaned close. "Eternal obedience," she cackled hysterically.

"What? Of all the ninnybrained notions—"

The raven jumped to her talons and started hopping around Doris in a dance of evil gloatingness. "Ninnybrained notions? Ninnybrained notions? Oh, no, Miss Gaudy, it ain't ninnybrained whatsoever. You see–" and her rough yellow tongue rolled out of her mouth to lick the drool from around the edges of her sharp beak– "in a few very short minutes, I am about to become a defecation."

Doris raised a featherbrow.

"Don't smirk like that at me with those coloured brows of yours! Craaaaarrrk! I am about to become a demi-god. How does *that* grab you, dolly-bird?"

"Like a bagful of wet porridge," Doris spat.

"And, seeing as how I'll be a demi-god and so important to the huge scheme of things in the new world as we will know it, I'll need someone to keep all of my disciples in check. Someone who will obey me for ever. That's where you come in, beautybeak."

"Never! I'll never serve you!"

"Oh, yes, you will. You'll have to. Because, you see, I'm going to pluck off all of your feathers, one by one, with my very own claws! Then I'm going to clip those wings of yours so you can't fly anywhere – you'll have to crawl, and hop, and go like a slug. And then you'll be so ugly to behold that the world will shun you. Nobody will come anywhere near you, you'll be so *repulsive*."

"You should be an expert on *that* situation."

"CRAAAARRRRK! Shut your beak. So it will be that I, Desdemona the Goddess of Vermin, shall take pity on you, the most pathetic form of vermin ever seen. And you shall serve me for evermore. Ha ha ha ha ha ha hahaha!"

Heavy footsteps interrupted her rantings. "Where in tarnation have you got to, you scrofulous sack of— Hellooo, what have we here?"

"I found some tinsel in the tree," croaked Desdemona.

"Arrr," purred Neptune Bone. The large, fleshy man stood towering over the gravestones, dressed the part for what was about to take place. He had torn the front of his Hermione Dinkus frock asunder, and was now wearing it over his shirt and emerald-green waistcoat and floral plus-fours trousers like a great, billowing, purple robe. In his pudgy hands he clasped the box containing the Sacred Alabastron of Cronus, with such a precious grip that it might very well have been his own heart in there.

"If I'm not very much mistaken – and I never have been, in my human existence – that bundle of birdlike boisterousness is known as 'Doris'. Are you not, bird?"

"Raaaarrrk!" screeched Doris.

Bone continued. "Where there's a Dorothea, there's usually a goody-goody member of my profession lurking. You've done very well, Desdemona. I may even promote

you to a demi-semi god if this all turns out the way—"

Heavier footsteps broke through the twigs and bushes. A huge white mass moved towards them.

"Ah, macho-boy." Bone addressed Herakles, who stood waiting before him. "Remain still for a few moments, we may be having visitors."

Herakles stood, watching. The moonlight bounced off his heavy features.

"REEERRRRRRRRRRRAAAAAARRRRRK!" screeched Doris, still firmly pinioned.

"That's right," Bone murmured, "keep up that noise, and your buddy-buddy will be here in no time at—"

"Doris! My dear, are you all right? Whoooaaa, Brenda!"

Bone's eyes lit up at the sight of Jim, Euripides and Brenda coming to a surprised halt.

"All of our chicks have come home to roost," crowed Desdemona.

"The fugitive brigade is here, all right," sneered Bone. "What's up, Cairo Jim? Is this the only place left to hide from the Antiquities Squad? Hmmmm?"

"Bone, you scoundrel!" Jim leapt off Brenda and came running to Doris's aid. "You ostentatious ruffian, you—"

"Seize them, Herakles!" Bone gestured quickly, and Herakles, understanding his order, moved forward.

Cairo Jim, Doris, Brenda and Euripides didn't have a chance.

▲ ▲ ▲

The stage had been set.

Bone had made Herakles place the altar from the Delphi Museum on the floor of the Anaktoron, near to the five standing marble columns. It was here that, in ancient times, the holy of holies stood, and where initiation ceremonies took place in the old religious orders.

Now Neptune Bone – wearing a purple fez (with a laurel wreath draped over it) to match his frock/robe – stood on the steps before the altar, his eyes glinting wildly.

High above, the clouds swirled, gathering speed and sometimes parting for a short while, to reveal scatterings of white, shining objects in their midst.

Bone looked over his shoulder at his captives. "That's it, Herakles, old chum. Keep 'em secure. But don't crush 'em. At least not yet. No, I want Cairo Jim to behold my Transformation and to tremble in awe. Aaaaaarrrrrrrrrrr!"

The strongman statue was sitting astride the kneeling Brenda, who was unable to move because of the immense weight. Under each of his arms, Herakles held Jim and Euripides as though they were bundles of squirming, wet clothing.

"Oh, I always said you were a genius," shrieked Desdemona, firmly gripping Doris in front of her in a vice-like winglock. Doris struggled, but the raven tightened her hold. "It's useless, macaw," she crowed. "We've got you in our clutches. Ha ha ha ha!"

"Jim!" Doris cried. "What'll we do?"

Cairo Jim took a deep breath, as Herakles' arm squeezed him more sharply. "I'm sorry, my dear, I ... I don't know."

"Oh, dear," moaned Euripides.

Even Brenda was at a loss for once in her Bactrian life. She lowered her head to the ground and snorted sadly.

Bone brought out his gold fob-watch from the pocket of his waistcoat. He snapped the cover open and held the timepiece so that it caught the moonlight. "Arrr," he whispered loudly. "Four minutes to the hour. Let us set up the props."

He bent over and picked up the small bronze Tripod of Tiphistiades. This he held out in front of him, turning slightly so that his captives could see it. "Let me give you a small running commentary," he sneered. "So that you all know precisely what is about to take place. You might like to think of it as my last great act of humanity and generosity before my Divinity becomes second nature."

He tenderly opened all three legs of the Tripod and placed it onto the altar, above the small, circular depression in the centre of the flat slab. "The Tripod must be placed directly over this small hollow. According to the book by that Helena Hattbocks, it is of vital importance that the positioning of the Tripod is exact. One millimetre out and the whole Divine Opening Ceremony will fail."

He grunted for a bit as he fiddled with the placement

of the Tripod. Then, when it was fixed to his satisfaction, he straightened and bent to the ground again. This time he opened the box containing the Sacred Alabastron of Cronus and, with the gentlest of chubby fingers, he held this aloft.

The moonlight picked it out and made it shimmer.

"And now, before time ticks cruelly away, I shall place the Sacred Alabastron of Cronus onto the top of the Tripod." He carefully did so, balancing it on the small brass platform on the Tripod's apex.

"The reason for all of this elaborate setting up? I shall tell you. The alabastron, you see, must from this moment onwards not, I repeat NOT, be touched by human hands. Only can the stopper in the top of the alabastron be touched, not the vessel itself. In order to release the stopper, however, and ultimately to release the great Titans themselves, the Sacred Alabastron must be sitting in the depression in the centre of the altar. Hence the Tripod. By carefully pulling out all three legs at the same time, the alabastron will be lowered, and I will be able to take out the stopper. Arrrrr!"

"Genius, genius, genius," chanted Desdemona hoarsely.

Bone looked once again at his fob-watch and, removing it from its chain, placed it on top of the altar so that he could keep his eye on it. "One minute to go."

He gave the biggest smirk of his life over his purple shoulder. "Arr, if only Mother could see me now.

Jocelyn Osgood, here I come!"

Cairo Jim blinked at the sound of his good friend's name. As he watched Captain Neptune Flannelbottom Bone wiping down his sweaty fingers prior to the lowering of the Tripod, and as he heard his own Cutterscrog timepiece ticking away loudly on his wrist, he was completely unaware of the persistent, clean shaft of moonlight that was shooting down onto the object on his own finger.

THE DIVINE OPENING CEREMONY

BONE DID HIS BEST to stop his hands from trembling as he gripped the tops of the legs of the Tripod of Tiphistiades. He glanced at his fob-watch. "Thirty seconds. Oh, goodbye, humanity, goodbye, Cairo Jim. For you and your friends, it shall be a goodbye *reeking* of finality!"

"Crark! Lower it, lower it!"

"No!" shouted Jim, the perspiration pouring from his forehead and into his eyes. "Bone, have some goodness, I beg you! If you're to open that alabastron all hell might break loose!"

"What a stimulating concept. Arrrrr."

Bone's eyes shone like a dragon's as he smoothly pushed the legs down. Out they splayed, each of them at the same angle, down, down, down, until at last they lay flat along the surface of the altar.

"Phew," Bone breathed. The Sacred Alabastron of Cronus now sat directly in the depression. Bone looked again at his fob-watch. "Five seconds till Kingdom Come!"

He took hold of the stopper between thumb and forefinger.

"Rarrrrk!" Doris screamed. "He's undoing it!"

Time swam about in front of Cairo Jim, as though every single fraction of a second around him had its own set of arms and legs, and was struggling, stroking, *kicking* against the current of air that made up the sea of all that was surrounding him. He was about to lose consciousness, when...

...There was a huge gust of wind above them all.

From out of the skies, at the very stroke of the beginning of midnight, a gigantic white figure swooped down and landed by the altar.

"Arrrrr," wailed Bone, startled by the sudden manifestation. He took his fingers from the stopper and stepped backwards, his eyes filling with the vision of this massively tall marble figure standing before him in a veil of glimmering light. She had no head or arms, but was clearly a woman; her voluminous robes folded about her curved form with rippling majesty; the enormous wings that rose from her back almost touched the very clouds themselves.

"Cairo Jim," Euripides gasped, hardly able to speak, "it is the Winged Victory of Samothrace! She has come back!"

Jim opened his eyes and looked up. The sight of her filled his heart so much he felt it would surely burst. "Nike herself," he whispered.

Brenda's eyes filled with astonishment.

Doris was absolutely squawkless.

The Winged Victory stood before Bone, and a breeze rose up and rustled through her white skirts, rippling them silently.

"And look," whispered Euripides. "In the skies, there are hundreds—no, *thousands*, of others. Statues everywhere, floating and bobbing."

Jim turned his eyes to the heavens and stared in wonder.

"No!" Bone reached out and snatched up the alabastron. "You think you have thwarted me?" he cried to Nike. "Not on your Nellie. The stopper might still be on, but I shall return tomorrow evening, when you, and all of your like, will have been eradicated! Then I shall go through this Ceremony once again."

"What does he mean, eradicated?" said Jim.

"In the meantime," Bone growled, "it's high time I brought out my own 'heavy artillery'!" He raised the Sacred Alabastron of Cronus to his lips and whispered at it. Then he smiled – a threatening, cruel snarl of a smile.

"What's happening?" Doris had by now got her voice back.

"Shut up, you technicolour twerp," Desdemona threatened.

All of the bushes behind them crashed and fell, and an infernal grinding cry filled the Sanctuary.

SSSSSCCCCHHHHHHRRRRRRRREEEEEEEEL-LLLLLLLKKKKK!

Towards the altar crashed Bone's "heavy artillery", knocking over loose pieces of the marble building as it advanced. It prowled slowly, but with menace in every step it took.

Jim had never seen anything like it moving before, but he knew immediately what it was: its sleek lion's body pulsating with sinewy muscles, its cruelly impassive human's face and rigid trellises of plaited hair, its arching, huge wings shooting out from its curved back and the powerful paws with their claws ready for springing could only belong to one creature.

"The Sphinx of the Naxians!" he gasped. "Bone stole it from the Delphi Museum!"

"The ancient strangler itself," whispered Euripides in terror.

The Sphinx of the Naxians settled itself on the marble floor of the Sanctuary, its long, whip-like tail slashing through the air and coming to rest against its squatting haunches.

"*RAAAARRRRRRRRK!*" Doris screeched.

"*CRAAARRRRRRRRK!*" Desdemona wailed, letting go of Doris, but too paralysed with fear to fly off.

"Seize her!" Bone gestured towards the colossal sphinx and then towards the Winged Victory.

The sphinx looked at Bone's hand, and slowly its head turned and followed the trail of his gesture. Its immovable eyes passed across Herakles and on to Nike. Then, as Bone scarpered to a far corner, the sphinx got to its feet and padded stealthily towards the beautiful Winged Victory.

"That's it," Bone whispered, a growl of fury in his throat. "Pulverize her! Pulverize her marble form to dust! Let me scatter her on the four winds myself! Arrrrr!"

The sphinx stood before Nike, looking into what would have been her face if she still had her head.

The grey and silver clouds overhead stopped swirling and became still.

All around them in the skies, the multitude of silent white marble forms and figures stopped their scattering, and waited motionless, suspended with the clouds.

The tail of the Sphinx of the Naxians rose, like a timid serpent, and closed back around its rear legs.

"Go on," hissed Bone. "What are you waiting for? Do her like a … *what?* What are you doing? *Nooooo!*"

The sphinx had turned. Now, with its eyes full of the pomp and glory of Captain Neptune Bone, it pounced through the still air – *SWOOSH* – and came to land right before the enrobed man himself.

"No, leave me alone, no, you can't, I'm too young to —WHOOOAAAAAAAAAA!"

The sphinx had him in its two front paws and, with a flap of its scroll-like wings, had risen into the air.

"Put me down, you marble leonine lump, let me go!"

But the creature flew off, far out to sea, where it soon became a blur against the night. Desdemona took off after it. "Hey, leave him alone. He's my master, my salvation … he's gonna make me a demi-god … come back here…"

Soon she, too, was a blur.

It was several minutes before anyone could speak. Then Jim said, kindly but with authority, "Herakles, arise."

Herakles felt the vibrations of Cairo Jim's words against his marble skin. Silently he stood, letting Jim and Euripides free and unencumbering Brenda from his weight.

"Quaaaooo," she snorted with relief.

Without a sound, this mighty man of marble walked towards Nike. He stood with her for a moment and then, with not a ripple, they both rose into the sky, to join their other sculpted companions in flight.

With as little fuss as they had made when they had arrived, the white figures of the countless statues were all borne away by the winds of the night.

The morning light came early that day.

After the last of the sky-bound statuary had departed, when the clouds had cleared and dissolved into a trillion wisps of memory, while Jim, Doris, Brenda and Euripides were still sitting in a dazed state, Euripides turned to his friends and made a small announcement.

"Do you know, I have learned something of absolute importance from all of this fantasticalness," he said proudly.

"Oh, yes?" said Jim.

"Yes. And not only from what has happened here around us last night. I have also learnt this thing of absolute importance from you and Miss Doris and Miss Brenda."

"And what," asked Jim, "might this thing of absolute importance *be*?"

Euripides smiled and scratched his right kneecap. "That *history* is not something to only keep locked away in museums and sunless places. I have discovered, with your help of course, that history is *alive*."

"You'll never speak a truer word, Euripides," Jim smiled. He reached out and tousled Doris's crestfeathers, then he reached over and gently rubbed Brenda's snout.

"'And flecked Darkness like a drunkard reels from forth Day's path and Titan's fiery wheels'", Doris quoted. "Rark. *Romeo and Juliet*, Act Two, Scene Three."

"Very good, Doris."

Brenda sent a telepathic thought. "Only One Kind of Man Will Bring You Good Fortune When You Seek The Forgotten' – what kind of man is that?"

Jim frowned for a second. "'Only One Kind of Man Will Bring You Good Fortune When You Seek The Forgotten'", he said. "Now why has that popped into my head all of a sudden?"

Brenda nudged the ring on his finger with her lips.

"I know," Doris hopped about happily. "I know the answer!"

"Go on, Doris," said Jim. "What is it?"

She looked at the ring. "A *talis*man, of course! Rark."

"A talisman," repeated Euripides Doodah. "How clever you all are."

The archaeologist-poet smiled. "My, oh my, what a wonderful day," he sighed, wearily but contentedly.

🔲🔲🔲🔲🔲 **22** 🔲🔲🔲🔲🔲

APOLLO SUMS IT UP

FROM THE CASEBOOK of Chief Inspector Reg Apollo of the Hellenic Branch of the Antiquities Squad:

There are many things about this whole case I have not been able to put my finger on, even now, four months after the event.

For the official record, Cairo Jim, Doris the macaw, Brenda the Wonder Camel and Euripides Doodah, Keeper of the Gallery of Forgotten Gods at the National Archaeological Museum in Athens, were never guilty of the crimes detailed elsewhere in this case.

It appears that Captain Neptune F. Bone, archaeologist and (severely unfinancial) Member of the Old Relics Society in Cairo, Egypt, was the guilty party. Aided by a raven answering to the name of "Desdemona", he carried out the various thefts and acts of gross vandalism which culminated in certain occurrences that took place on the evening in question at the Sanctuary of the Great Gods at Samothraki.

What has happened to Bone? When last seen by me, from my vantage point on a cliff by the

Sanctuary of the Great Gods, he was being carried out to sea by some huge, winged creature. Looking through my night-vision binoculars, this creature bore a striking resemblance to the statue known as the Sphinx of the Naxians, which was stolen some time earlier from the Museum at Delphi.

As I watched them disappearing, I observed that a small object – possibly a vase of some sort – spilled from his hand and fell into the waters far below. About a minute after this, a fluttering smudge became visible. It appeared to be menacing the sphinx-like creature, and it continued to do so, almost dive-bombing the thing, until the sphinx (or whatever it was) let go of Bone and let him, too, fall into the ocean's depths.

The creature then appeared to fly off, empty-taloned, in a westerly direction.

Neither Captain Neptune Bone nor his companion raven have been seen or heard from since this incident.

Perhaps the strangest thing about the whole case is this: on the morning after the night in question, I received a report from Head Office of the Antiquities Squad that the steps of the National Archaeological Museum in Athens were filled with ancient Greek statuary. The seven thousand or so items seemed to have been dumped there; by

whom we know not. Many of the items have been catalogued as having been missing for long periods of time; some of them for hundreds of years.

How they came to be there, I can only wonder. I dare say I shall still be wondering about it until my dying day.

(signed) Chief Inspector Reg Apollo.

THE END

Swoggle me sideways! Unearth more thrilling mysteries of history starring Cairo Jim, Doris, and Brenda the Wonder Camel – **THE CAIRO JIM CHRONICLES**

CAIRO JIM ON THE TRAIL TO CHACHA MUCHOS

Why did an ancient Peruvian tribe dance themselves to death? Can that well-known archaeologist and little-known poet Cairo Jim uncover the secrets of ChaCha Muchos before the evil Captain Bone? And will Jim *ever* get any poetry published... Find out in his first flabbergasting adventure!

CAIRO JIM IN SEARCH OF MARTENARTEN

Does the lost tomb of Pharaoh Martenarten spell doom for Cairo Jim? What lies beyond the Door of Death? Could it, in fact, be doom? And is the world really ready for a pigeon-based fast food chain... Find out in the second scintillating tale of Cairo Jim!

CAIRO JIM AND THE SUNKEN SARCOPHAGUS OF SEKHERET

What sinister secrets lie hidden in the depths of the Red Sea? Will evil genius Captain Bone's greed for gold lead him to a watery grave? Has Cairo Jim's flabber finally been gasted? All will be revealed in his third flummoxing exploit!

The Cairo Jim Chronicles, read by Geoffrey McSkimming, are available on CD from Bolinda Audio Books! See **www.bolinda.com** for details.